DADDY'S GIRL

AN AGE GAP SURPRISE PREGNANCY ROMANCE

K.C. CROWNE

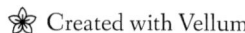

DESCRIPTION

She desperately needs a fiancé. So I'll pretend.
How can I object to the gorgeous virgin who walks into my strip club?
She thinks this is an escort service - and that I'm for hire.
Damn is she in the wrong place.

We're nothing alike.
Delilah is a family girl. Pure. Gentle.
I'm an arrogant prick and I take what I want.
Right now, I want her.
She arouses parts of me I've had locked away for years.
So, I'll play the role of a loving fiancé.
Caress and kiss her in all the right ways.
And when we're alone...
I'll claim that sweet innocence.
Make her mine.
Feel her body tremble and beg for more.

I don't want it to end. And that was the last thing I expected.
After all of this history she'll have more than just memories.
I have a special gift in store for Delilah.

CHAPTER 1

DELILAH

"Are you even listening to me?"

I couldn't focus my attention on anything my best friend Laura yelled at me as she zipped across the apartment, tossing clothes and shoes in my direction that she wanted me to try on.

My eyes were locked onto the screen of my MacBook. Specifically, the enormous amount of money that, in a few months, was going to be mine.

I couldn't wrap my head around it. After spending the past three years living hand-to-mouth as I struggled to balance work and college, I was about to be rich.

The moment I turned twenty-one, I'd have access to the trust fund that my grandparents had established for me before they passed.

"Come *on!*" Laura poked her head out of the bathroom, a frazzled, frustrated look on her face. Laura was pretty. Tall, leggy and blonde, she'd always been the type to turn heads.

Tonight, that was exactly what she wanted to do.

"OK, ok! One sec."

She came out of the bathroom dressed in a tight, dark blue cocktail dress that showed off just about every curve of her yoga sculpted body. She rushed over with surprising speed in her heels to where I was seated on the edge of the bed.

"Don't tell me you're watching more cooking videos on TikTok. I swear, you—" she stopped herself midsentence when she saw what I was looking at. "Come on – *again*?"

I wasn't even going to bother defending myself. "I can't help it! It's...so weird."

"I know it's weird. But I don't get why you're stressing out about it so much. In three months, you're going to have so much money that you won't even know what do with it." She pointed a finger at me, her dark eyebrows raised. "Which is a huge problem if you ask me. If I had this kind of trust fund, I know exactly the first thing I'd be doing with it. I'll give you a hint – it starts with 'B' and ends with '-irkin'."

I couldn't help but laugh. Laura was lighthearted and had a way of breaking apart tense situations whenever they came up. The total opposite of my tendency to overthink and get lost in my own head.

We'd been friends since we were kids and had always complemented one another.

"It's not that simple. Last weekend I had to overdraft my account just so I could buy groceries for the week. Until my paycheck went through, I not only had no money, but *negative* money."

Laura gave me a confused look, as if she weren't sure of what to make of my comment.

"Here, I know what you need." She got up and made her way over to the small kitchen of her apartment. I watched as she opened the fridge and pulled out a bottle of Rose'. "Keep talking! I'm listening!"

I sighed, running my hand through my wavy, brown hair.

"And now...I'm going to have more than enough money."

Two glasses of Rose' in hand, Laura came back over and sat down. She held out one of the glasses and I took it.

"You know what's going on here?" she asked. "You're thinking too much. And I know that because you've been thinking too much ever since we were kids."

"Yeah, I get it. But you don't think that a situation like this is something that necessitates a little thought?"

"Sure. But it hasn't even happened yet. In a few months you're going to have a lot of money. But for now, you're the same old Delilah Kline with a negative balance in her bank account and nothing else to worry about besides getting out the door and going to this party in West Hollywood with me and having the time of your life."

With her free hand, she closed the laptop and tossed it onto her bed.

"I swear, for someone who lives in Silver Lake, you're not taking advantage of the amazing party potential of LA *at all*. You're either at school or working at the coffee shop or with your nose buried in whatever biology textbook you're studying. You need to live a little! Lucky for you, you've got a best friend who always knows where the best parties in town are."

She grinned that wide, toothy smile that she'd been using to win people over since she was a little girl.

"And that's what you should be thinking about tonight – not what you're going to do with money you don't even have yet. Besides, you're probably the most responsible person I know. *Too* responsible if you ask me. I don't have any doubt that you'll figure out what you want to do with it."

Hearing Laura's vote of confidence went a long way. However, it wasn't just the responsibility of having tons of money at my disposal that I was worried about.

"Thanks. But it's Mom that's really on my mind."

"Oh no. What's she doing?"

"She's doing exactly what you think a woman who somehow managed to get knocked up by some guy at the age of forty-five is doing – she's hitting me up."

Laura sighed and shook her head. Up until that moment she'd been giving me the business, performing her usual role of trying to get me to stop overthink things. The mere mention of my mom was enough to get her to switch over to total empathy mode.

Ever since Dad died when I was a kid, I'd had to deal with Mom and her antics. So many of my childhood memories were of Mom coming home drunk after a night out at some Hollywood bar, her sleazeball-of-the-week on her arm.

Sleazy guys who had no qualms about eyeing up Laura and me while we were barely in our teens.

Mom didn't care.

Her life was about fun and having as few responsibilities as possible. The guy she'd been currently shacking up with seemed to be on the more straight and narrow, but I still didn't have any faith that my mother had changed her ways.

In true irresponsible form, Mom wanted it both ways. Her life of ignoring me and bed hopping her way across the greater LA metro area had left her without a penny to her name.

She'd known, however, that my grandparents on Dad's side had set aside healthy trusts for my two sisters and me.

Mom wanted at them. She had a new baby, after all.

"It's insane," Laura said. "Like, how little shame do you have to have to do something like that?"

Despite Laura being a girl who never missed a party, she had a damn good head on her shoulders. We were close enough that I'd trusted her to be able to be honest about my mom.

"Mom and shame don't even live on the same continent. Here, look at this."

I lifted the right side of my butt up enough to reach into my pocket and slip out my phone. I pulled up the series of texts I'd received from my mom over the last week or so.

I hadn't replied to any of them. I handed the phone over to Laura, who eagerly snatched it from my hand and began reading.

After a minute or so of her scanning through the texts, she shook her head in disbelief.

"Wow. These are ... God, I don't even know what to say about them. So, the one where she throws a pity party about how she needs a little help to pay for her medication ..."

I knew exactly the text she was talking about and let out a laugh at the mere mention of it.

"Please. The only 'medication' Mom's on is her weekly bottle of Tito's."

Laura laughed, turning her attention back to my phone. "She seems to get the hint that playing the victim card isn't going to work that well. Damn, she really runs the gamut of emotions – there's pity to guilt then anger then threatening to never speak to you again."

"See what I mean? Totally shameless. Maybe if I were thirteen again that kind of crap would work. But not now. It's all just her trying one angle after another to get what she wants."

"And what she wants is *your* money. What a load of crap."

I nodded. Laura always had my back.

"You got it."

Laura sipped her wine. "Wait, what about your sisters?"

I was the middle of three sisters, Maryann three years older than me and Corrine two years younger. Both were experts in the sort of manipulation and mind games in which Mom had always excelled.

"Mom hounded Maryann when she was my age. She wanted the money like crazy, and only backed off when Maryann told her she was leaving the money in the trust and wouldn't be touching it for years, since she had her own job and own source of income. Corrine's been watching this current mess play out and is starting to wonder what she's going to be in for when she turns twenty-one. But what can they do, you know? It's my money, and my problem."

"Then there's the matter of the one your mom just had..."

"Yeah. That's the hard part." I sipped my wine, suddenly needing it badly. "I want to help my new sister – I really do. Knowing she's going to be all alone dealing with my mom once she runs off the father like I'm sure she will, my sister is going to need every advantage she can get. And my money would be a huge one."

"But it'd still have to go through your mom."

"Right. And there's not a chance in hell I'd trust her to use the money responsibly. She'd show up in all Fendi everything and maybe kick a few dollars to my sister for formula and diapers. What I need to do is stand up to Mom, but I have no idea how. Whenever I try to confront her, she knows how to push my buttons, how to flip the script and get me so worked up that I can't back her off and I just end up sounding as crazy as she is."

I sighed, the weight of the situation taking hold.

"God, I'm sorry, I'm being a total vibe crusher before we're supposed to go out and have fun."

Laura said nothing. Instead, she stared forward with her brow scrunched, as if she were deep in thought.

"Uh, you OK?"

Laura nodded. "I'm thinking we should skip the party tonight."

"Wait, what? Why?"

A mischievous expression flashed across her face, one that I'd seen many times before. "I have an idea that could solve your problem."

"You do?"

"Yep. Listen, I know you're more than capable of standing up to your mom, but a little backup wouldn't hurt Someone that'll put her back on her heels a bit; shake her up."

I was so confused that all I could muster in response was a "huh?"

Her grin spread. "There's this club that I went to a couple of Fridays ago."

"A *club*? Why do I get the impression that there's something more to it than you're letting on?"

"Well, because there is. It's a strip club, and—"

"Wait, wait, wait," I waved my hands in front of my face. "Why were you at a strip club?"

Laura shrugged, as if it were no big deal.

"I was out on a date with that guy Vassily. Remember him? Like six-foot-five, built like a tank, covered in tattoos ..." she trailed off as she spoke, biting down on her lower lip as she thought of the man in question.

"Focus," I said with a smile.

She quickly shook her head, coming back to the moment. "Sorry – got a little, uh, distracted. Anyway, one night we were out for drinks, and I asked if he had any ideas for someplace interesting to go, somewhere out of the ordinary. He got this wicked look on his face and said he knew just the place."

"So, we get into his Bugatti and drive down to this weird spot in West Hollywood. The door to enter the club was in an alley and there was a password to get in. It was like a movie. We go down this hall and the whole time I'm wondering what the hell I've gotten myself into."

"At the end of the hall you could hear music beyond another door. It was bizarre Delilah. The most beautiful men and women you've ever seen were everywhere."

"So, like a high-end strip club?" I asked.

"Yeah, you could say that. The customers were loaded. As in bottles of Cristal and Ben Franklin's flying around like dollar bills. It was crazy."

I was intrigued. Laura was the kind of girl who'd been around; she was no stranger to fancy Hollywood parties and guys with plenty of cash and pull around town. So, when I noticed her demeanor getting more serious as she told the story, I knew I needed to pay close attention.

Part of me wanted to stop the conversation in its tracks, to tell Laura that whatever she was leading up to, I wasn't interested.

However, I didn't do that. Instead, I told her to go on.

"Anyway, this place caters to all sorts of men. The majority are rich and powerful, but I'm also talking about the entourages of these guys, their bodyguards and security, guys looking to make a name for themselves. I bet one of them would be more than happy to help you out."

"Wait, what? How do you mean 'help me out'?"

She grinned. "With your little problem."

"Please tell me you're not suggesting I hire some MMA slash part-time bodyguard to beat up my mom."

Laura laughed. "Nothing so dramatic. Here's what I'm thinking. You've got some money saved up from your job on campus, right?"

"Well, yeah, a little."

"Great. So, take that money, find one of these guys, and tell him you need someone to pretend to be your fiancé."

"My *what?*" I couldn't believe what I was hearing.

She raised her palms.

"Hear me out. You tell him you need someone to pretend to be your fiancé, that you need him to come with you to meet your mom. I know this sounds insane but trust me. You tell your mom that he's a whiz with money, that he's going to help you handle your finances when it comes to your trust."

I immediately wanted to protest, to say that it was simply too insane to consider. At the same time, I could sense where she was going with it.

"You've always had a problem with your mom getting you super worked up right?"

"Yeah. It doesn't matter what I tell myself before we talk, or how much I psyche myself up. She always knows exactly what to say to push my buttons."

Laura nodded.

"Now, imagine those meetings if you've got some gigantic guy with tattoos and a shaved head next to you, who's totally intimidating and happens to know his way around an account book. Your mom wouldn't have a leg to stand on when it came to trying to get your money."

I sighed. The plan was insane, but it made a certain amount of sense. All I'd need is a couple meetings with Mom to set her straight.

Not to mention, I was out of options. I'd have access to my money soon, but if I didn't have Mom squared away before then, she'd make my life a living hell.

"But I don't have that much money saved up. Is this hypothetical guy going to go to all this trouble for the twenty-two hundred dollars I have in my savings?"

"Um, you're about to have access to your millionaire grandparents' trust fund! Tell him your story and give him two thousand as a down payment."

I couldn't believe I was even considering it. The plan was nuts, far-fetched, and maybe even a little dangerous. Despite all that, all I could say was...

"Alright, fine. Let's do it."

CHAPTER 2

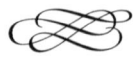

JACOB

The low pulsing of dance music.
  The bite of whiskey on my tongue.
The smell of sex in the air.
All signs that it was going to be a good night at the club.
My club.
"Another pour, Mr. Nichols?"
I pulled my eyes away from the writhing masses on the dance floor and turned slowly in the direction of the voice. It belonged to Sean, one of my bartenders.
He held a bottle of Macallan in his hands, my drink of choice, and the expression on his face mirrored the rest of my staff - that perfect blend of respect and fear.
I glanced down at my glass, noticing it was a little low.
"Yes, Sean. Another pour."
He nodded, taking the glass, and poured a splash of booze inside. My bartenders always poured me a bit extra than standard. While I appreciated the sentiment, it was a bit early in the night to get too stupefied off good scotch. I raised a palm signaling for him to stop.

The night was young, and I wanted to be sharp. Who knew what the hours ahead would hold?

When the glass was in front of me once more, I turned back around in my seat and took in the scene.

My club, Cherry Lane, was one of the, if not *the*, most exclusive gentlemen's clubs in Los Angeles. The women were the most beautiful in the world, the men some of the wealthiest and most powerful.

Cherry Lane was a place such men could come to relax and unwind, to soak up the sights of gorgeous girls dancing for them and them alone.

Phones were not permitted inside, and anyone allowed into the club was checked then double-checked to make certain they were the sort to be trusted.

Those who knew my name knew damn well that trust was a gift I only gave once.

The club was three stories, with plenty of room for both dancing and booths where guests could sit and drink and engage in quiet conversation.

Women wearing barely anything at all twisted their lithe bodies around golden poles, while wealthy men and their hulking bodyguards watched them with pleased, but reserved, expressions.

More than a few women in the mass of bodies on the dance floor made eyes at me, flashing their most seductive looks letting me know that they were there for the taking, should I want them.

It was easy enough to simply meet their expressions with a smile of wry amusement before turning my attention elsewhere. While I considered myself a connoisseur of female beauty, I was a businessman first and foremost.

Sometimes I caught myself wondering if I was getting burned out. Other times I considered that my standards were only getting higher.

Either way, I didn't worry about it a bit – worrying had never been my style.

Sipping my drink, the buzzing of my phone in my pocket called my attention.

It was a text from Archie Doggett, my body man.

We have a situation. VIP room five.

Archie worked directly underneath me, the man in charge of all day-to-day club matters, including those of security.

While the buck stopped with me, I trusted him enough to handle the daily decisions required to successfully run a club like mine.

If he was asking for my personal attention with an issue, that meant it was something serious. I pushed my drink away and stood up.

More gazes latched onto me as I rose, as if they were hoping that I'd chosen one of them for some special attention.

Sexual matters were the last thing on my mind at that moment. My club came first – no matter what.

I moved through the crowd, the patrons parting around me as soon as they glanced up and realize who I was. It took no time at all for me to arrive at the private elevator that led to the upper floors.

Upon reaching the third floor, the doors opened, revealing a long hallway guarded by two hulking men in suits.

The third floor was the most exclusive providing space for the VIP rooms where guests could speak in total privacy for whatever reasonable purpose they desired.

The guards stepped aside as I approached. I blew past them, soon reaching the VIP room in question.

The door was nondescript, nothing but a small "5" in an ornate font near the doorknob. Without knocking, I turned the knob and stepped inside.

The room was large, adorned with plush seating and soft lighting, low electronic music playing throughout.

"I paid for her, and that means I get to do whatever the hell I want."

The voice of Anatoly Petrovitch, one of the wealthiest men on the planet, greeted me as I stepped into the room. The older man was dressed in one of his usual expensive suits, the jacket off and tie undone.

One look at him, along with the half-empty bottle of expensive vodka close at hand, let me know he'd been overindulging.

Behind him sat Clarissa, one of the newest hires at Cherry Lane. Clarissa was a beautiful redheaded girl, just a few months past her twenty-first birthday.

She was dressed in a skintight, dark red cocktail dress, her hair was mussed, and her arms were defensively folded over her chest. An expression of worry and fear on her face was plain to see.

The redness around her right wrist resembling a handprint was also plain to see.

Archie was on the other side of the room. He was tall, with a shaved head that showed off the tattoo of a cobra behind his ear - a holdover from his days in the Irish Mafia.

Archie had the look of a man you didn't want to mess with, his face sharp and aggressive, his dark eyes narrow and piercing, his build enormous.

Behind his hunter's eyes was a scheming and brilliant mind – just the sort of man you wanted as your right hand.

All eyes locked onto me as soon as I stepped into the room.

"What the hell is going on here?" I already had a pretty good idea, but I wanted to hear it firsthand.

"Ah, Mr. Nichols." Anatoly's demeanor changed as soon as I spoke, taking a much more respectful tone.

"Finally, you arrive to sort this matter out. Let me explain to you what is—"

I held up my finger. "Not a word. Archie, fill me in."

Anatoly's face flashed with anger and confusion. Clearly, he wasn't used to being dismissed.

In my club, the rules were different.

"Evidently, Anatoly here—"

"That's *Mr. Petrovitch*, to you."

Archie let out an amused snort. "Yeah, sure, Mr. Petrovitch.

Anyway, he brought Clarissa up here for some one-on-one time and is now pissed about how it worked out for him."

I turned to Clarissa. "You OK?"

She nodded slowly, pursing her lips. It was clear that she was afraid of sharing too much, of getting on Anatoly's bad side. The man was a powerful billionaire.

"I'm fine."

She wasn't fine. Far from it.

I was pissed.

I stepped over to her, offering my hand to help her up. I leaned and quietly spoke into her ear.

"You're under my protection. Don't be afraid to tell the truth."

She regarded me with an expression of confusion, as if she wasn't sure she'd heard me correctly. I nodded, letting her know that I was serious.

Clarissa closed her eyes and spoke.

"He said he wanted me to come to a VIP room for some private time, said that he'd pay me for it. As soon as the door shut, he...he started putting his hands all over me. I told him to stop, but he wouldn't. Then he grabbed me by the wrist and shoved me. That's when I pressed the button to call for help."

Each VIP room in the club had a hidden button for this exact situation, to alert the guards and let them know the girl, or girls, inside needed help.

"You're a lying bitch," Anatoly snarled. "I didn't touch you."

I kept my voice calm and maintained my poise. "Each room has a security feed. If there's a dispute, we'll review the tapes and confirm which of you is telling the truth and which one isn't."

My money was on Clarissa. Rich men believing they could do whatever they wanted and get away with it was a tale as old as time – especially in my line of work.

Anatoly's eyes flashed. "You record everything that happens in here?"

"Of course," I said. "We don't have the feed on active displays, but it's still being recorded. Very useful when disputes like this occur."

Anatoly clearly hadn't planned on this. Or, perhaps, he was simply too drunk and too arrogant to have the foresight. Either way, it was looking like my intuition had proved me right yet again.

"This little slut led me on!" he shouted, pointing at her behind him.

"What the hell did she think I meant when I offered to bring her up here for some one-on-one time? How stupid can you be?"

I took one, slow step closer to him.

"Watch your mouth, Anatoly. No one talks to my employees like that."

Chastened by my words, his lips formed a thin line.

"Now, you put your hands on her. Don't lie to me and tell me you didn't – I can see it on her wrist. You've been here enough times to know that's clearly against the rules. As of this moment, your membership at Cherry Lane is hereby revoked."

Judging by the rage that flashed across his face, Anatoly clearly hadn't been expecting this turn of events.

"What?" He spun around, turning to Clarissa. "This is all *your* fault!"

Anatoly made two miscalculations.

First, he moved toward Clarissa in a threatening manner. I quickly stepped in, positioning myself between the two of them and grabbing him by the collar of his very expensive dress shirt.

Then he made his second miscalculation – putting his hands on me.

"Get your fucking hands off of me!" he hissed.

He pulled his fist back to strike and my training kicked in. I pivoted to the side, easily dodging his sloppy, drunk punch.

As a three-time Olympic medal winning boxer, I easily had the skills to restrain him and end the fight right then and there. A quick step to his back followed by an arm lock would've done the job just fine.

However, he'd put his hands on one of my employees. For that, he needed to learn a lesson.

Anatoly recovered from his missed swing and prepared for another go.

I didn't give him the chance.

I raised my fist and gave him a quick jab, hard enough to send him staggering backward. Clarissa let out a shriek, but by then the fight was long over.

Just like I'd planned, Anatoly staggered toward Archie, who easily caught and restrained him. I'd hit the billionaire just hard enough to daze him, but not enough to do any real damage.

The situation over, I turned to Clarissa. "You alright?"

Her eyes wide, she nodded. "Yeah. I think so."

"Good. Take an hour."

Another nod. "Th-thank you."

I turned to Archie as Clarissa left the room.

"What about him, boss?"

I looked Anatoly up and down. Then I stepped to the door, poked my head out, and called for the guards.

"Take this asshole out back. He says anything, remind him that he's been banned. If he's got a problem with that, he can take it up with me."

Obeying without a word, they took Anatoly out of Archie's grip and carried him off to the elevator. Once they were gone, Archie sucked in a breath and shook his head.

"That's a bold move, boss."

"Bold or not, it needed to be done. Not a chance in hell I allow anyone like that in my club."

We started down the hall toward the elevator.

"He's going to sober up and realize what happened. Bet you anything he comes at you with fangs bared."

I couldn't help but grin. As much as I tried to be an even-keeled man of business, every now and then the fighter in me craved a challenge.

The elevator doors opened, and we stepped inside.

"You don't get to be a billionaire without having a little bit of sense," I said. "But if he wants to start something, let him. Might be entertaining."

Archie chuckled as the doors shut. "Where to, boss?"

"Top floor. I want to check the cameras to make sure Anatoly gets his ass off my property."

Archie nodded and pressed the button, the elevator rising and the doors opening with a chime a few moments later.

We headed down the hall and stepped through the door of the security room. The guard on duty looked up from the bank of CCTV screens, all of them tuned to various points in the club.

"Bring up the back alley," I said.

The guard did as I asked, typing in a few keys, and pulling up the camera feed from the alley behind the club.

I kept my eyes on it and, sure enough, before too long the door opened and the guards, along with their billionaire cargo, stepped out.

I watched as Anatoly was unceremoniously dumped onto the ground, the guards checking on him to make sure he was breathing, then leaving seconds later.

We continued to watch as Anatoly lifted himself up to look around and realize where he was. Then he took out his phone and made a call, a car arriving a few moments later. He hurried in and was gone.

"So far, so good," Archie said. "Now, we'll see if half the Russian Mafia doesn't show up tomorrow."

A chime sounded, and out of the corner of my eye I watched as Archie took his phone out of his pocket and checked the screen.

"Hm."

I glanced over. "What is it?"

"Couple of women trying to get in. They're not on the list." He flicked his eyes over to me. "You want me to send 'em packing?"

It was a situation that required a bit of thought. If it were a pair of men, the answer would be easy – deny entry, boot their asses out, maybe rough them up a bit so they would learn what happens when you're not on the list.

The fact that it was women...well, that was another matter altogether. Though my club was very exclusive, it was a club, nonetheless. That meant women were always welcome.

Not to mention, I always had my eyes open for new talent.

"Bring the entry hall camera up on the feed."

The guard nodded, then complied. The camera switched over to the entry hall, and sure enough, two women were on the screen.

What I saw was enough to take my breath away.

Both women were young and gorgeous.

The first was a blonde, while pretty enough, she was a type that we had more than enough of at the club.

The other woman was something else entirely. Calling her gorgeous was almost doing her a disservice.

She was slender but curvy, with curly, chocolate colored hair, a pert nose, and small, full lips. Her skin was fair and, despite the skintight dress she had on, she stood with her arms wrapped over her middle, as if she weren't entirely comfortable being there.

Everything about her shouted innocence. My cock twitched at the mere sight of her, and suddenly I yearned to take her, to make her mine.

"Hey, Mr. J?" Archie's voice snapped me back into the moment. "What do you want me to do with these two?"

I cleared my throat and stood up, adjusting my tie.

"Let them in. I want to give them a personal welcome."

CHAPTER 3

DELILAH

"Oh my God," Laura said, excitement in her eyes. "I can't wait to get back in here. It's...I don't even know how to say it, this place is like nowhere else in the world."

This is a huge mistake.

The thought appeared in my mind repeatedly, increasing in intensity with each step I took down the long hallway.

The space was strange - the hallway was illuminated by warm, track lighting and paintings of flowers that resembled a certain part of the female anatomy adorned the walls.

The door on the far end of the hall was nothing special, other than a small set of cherries illuminated with red neon light hanging above it.

If I'd been there alone with no idea of what to expect, I would've had a hard time summoning up the desire to keep going.

With Laura there by my side however, I could manage. All the same I felt completely out of my element standing there in front of the door, the pulsing club music on the other side.

"OK, I'm trying to remember what Vassily did," I heard Laura say. "There was like a password or a secret knock or something. But I was so excited at the time that I can't remember what it was."

I was having a hard time paying attention to her.

What *did* have my attention was the small camera in the corner of the hall, the little black dome that made me feel that it was looking directly at me and only me. I couldn't help but wonder who was on the other side.

Click.

"Whoa," the word tumbled out of Laura's mouth dripping with disbelief.

The door opened slowly, the volume of the music getting louder with every inch of space.

"Did we just get let in?" I asked, glancing over at my friend.

Laura reached forward and put her hand on the door, as if she were seeing things.

"It looks that way."

"Why would they just let us in like that?"

Laura was just as confused as I was, but the perplexed expression on her face quickly vanished, replaced by one of eager excitement.

"You kidding? Look at us! What club *wouldn't* want two girls like you and me in it?"

"One that doesn't know we're both under twenty-one, probably."

"Oh, they don't care about that. Come on!"

Without another word, Laura pulled open the door. There was one more hallway on the other side, this one just as minimal, but with electronic sensors on the walls.

I recognized the equipment right away.

"This is X-ray stuff," I said. "I remember seeing it in the labs at the bio department at school."

"X-ray? Oh, that's what this is? I remember thinking it was weird the first time I was here. Geez, I wonder what kind of clientele they have coming here if they want to make sure they're not packing or whatever."

I paused. "You sure you don't want to just go, head back home?"

"Not a chance," she said without a moment's hesitation. "You seriously think I'm going to let you come all this way only to turn back at the last minute? Besides, you need a solution to this little mother problem of yours, and I've got a damn good feeling that you're going to find it behind this door."

She flashed me a grin, and without another word, hurried to the door on the far end of the hallway.

I arrived at Laura's side right as she opened the door and was greeted with a sight that was unlike anything I'd seen before.

The club appeared to be three stories high as far as I could tell. The interior shape was a huge square, the walls lined with private booths, a massive dance floor in the center, bodies packed in tight and writhing to the music pulsing from the huge speakers next to the DJ booth on the far end.

White and red lights cut through the misty air of the space. The main décor was another set of neon cherries, just like I'd seen above the door when we'd first arrived, but these were gigantic, easily a dozen feet tall, and hung over the DJ booth.

"Holy shit," I said under my breath. "This is intense."

There were so many women, all of them stunning.

On the dance floor were women of all ethnicities dressed in tight skirts with low-cut tops and skintight dresses. The waitresses were clad in bikinis or lingerie as they hurried drinks here and there, moving quickly but seductively at the same time.

Some people sat in booths enjoying their cocktails and watching their surroundings while onlookers from the balcony above gazed down. I was overwhelmed, not sure what to do with myself.

Hulking guards in suits, guns displayed prominently at their hips, stood watch throughout. Though they all wore sunglasses even in the dark of the club, I felt as if their gazes were all on me.

"What do you even do at a place like this?" I asked, looking around.

"You have fun!" Laura replied as if that were the most obvious answer in the world.

"You're going to have to be more specific than that."

"Well, first thing's first – we're here on a mission. Now, this place has tons of guys here, as you can see. Look in the booths and take notice of what the set up is."

"The set up?"

"Yeah. Look around."

We moved further into the club, but before I could look around, I slammed into something – some*one*.

I looked up to see a tall, gorgeous woman in front of me with shimmering blonde hair and boobs so big and fake they looked on the verge of busting out of her low-cut dress. She was flanked by two other women, both just as stunning as she was.

She appeared surprised at first, then gazed down at me with a look of total disdain.

"Wow, they're letting anyone in here these days, huh?"

I might've been out of my element, but I wasn't about to let someone talk to me like that.

"Excuse me?" I asked.

"You heard me." She glanced over at Laura. "Did your friend bring you here to be nice?"

I narrowed my eyes. "You know, you're lucky I wasn't carrying a fork when I bumped into you. I might've accidentally popped those things."

Surprise flashed on the woman's face, and one of her friends chuckled.

"You'd better be careful what you say, or—"

"Or what? You'll topple over and crush me with an industrial load of silicone?"

Another laugh from one of her friends that was instantly met with a hard look from the woman standing in front of me.

Turning her attention back on me she hissed, "Listen, you scrawny-ass little loser, all I need to do is say one word to the guy I'm here with and—"

That was all she got out before Laura clamped her hand down on my shoulder and led me away.

"No need for a fight," she said over her shoulder. "All friends here!"

Her plan worked, and soon Laura and I had melted into the crowd, and I could no longer see the woman or her friends. Moments later, we were on the other side of the mass of people, my heart racing from the confrontation.

"OK," Laura said once we were clear. "Let's try not to get on the bad side of anyone within five minutes of showing up, alright?"

"Hey, she had it coming."

"Oh, I'm on your side. And if this were any other night, I'd be in her face right along with you. But we're here on a mission, remember? We need to think strategically. Now, remember what I was saying about the people in the booths? Look around."

It didn't take me long to see what she was talking about.

The men in the booths exuded power, money, and influence. Women hung on them, and large tattooed bodyguards stood close by, ever vigilant.

"Nothing but rich guys and their muscle," I said.

"That's right." Laura nodded, pleased that I understood what she'd been referring to. "So, all we have to do is pick out one of these guys and see if he's down!"

"God, you make it sound so simple. Like, 'hey, giant bodyguard? If I give you my money from the tip jar at my coffeeshop, will you help get my greedy mom off my back'?"

Laura laughed. "You're giving them more money than that. Trust me, they might think it's funny at first, but once you start hinting about the ballpark amount of your inheritance, they'll start taking you seriously right away."

"That reminds me, we must be cautious and find someone trustworthy. Last thing I want to do is get linked up with a guy who's going to scam me."

"You won't have to worry about that – these guys are the best of the best. Vassily was talking with a few of them and they're all ex-military types – with codes of honor and stuff. You don't get to this level of work unless you're someone the boss feels they can trust."

She was making a good case. However, there was still the matter of going through with it.

I opened my mouth to ask Laura what the next step was, but before I could say a word, I felt a huge hand on my shoulder.

I spun around and was greeted with the wide span of an enormous man's chest. I looked up to see that one of the guards was looming over me, his eyes looking down and locked onto mine.

In that moment, I was certain we were busted, that this guy had somehow realized that we were underage, and he'd come to throw us out on our asses.

He didn't say anything at first, and neither did we. The guard merely looked us up and down, sizing us up.

"Someone wants to speak with you." His voice was so deep that I could practically feel the reverberations in my bones.

"Someone wants to speak with *us*?" Laura put her hands on her hips and stepped right up to the guy. There wasn't a trace of fear in her words. "Who?"

The guard shared the same sentiment. "Member of the staff."

He swept his massive, meaty hand toward a booth in the corner, one so secluded that I wouldn't have noticed it if it hadn't been pointed out.

"OK," Laura said. "And why does that matter to us?"

"Laura!" I hissed.

"Because neither of you are supposed to be here. Now, either take a seat, or get moving." He swept his hand once more, this time toward the entrance.

We'd been busted, and while there was still some fear in me, I'd decided that I'd come too far to leave empty-handed. Laura put her hand on my wrist and leaned in.

"We can go," she whispered. "I didn't bring you here to get cornered by some goon like this."

While I was glad she was giving me an out, I shook my head.

"No. Let's see what this staff member wants."

Laura let go of my wrist and stepped back.

The guard, realizing that we were ready to follow him, turned and lead us into the booth.

I slid into the plush, red seat and noticed that the booth allowed for a nearly complete view of the club, all the way up to the third floor. In fact, seated there I could see that there were actually four floors to the club, a trio of large, square, black windows looking down from above.

"One moment, he will be right with you."

The guard left without another word, leaving Laura and I to wonder who this "he" was. Laura turned to me, her eyes flashing with excitement.

"This is insane. Who the hell is this person who wants to meet us so badly?"

She gasped. "What if it's one of those super rich oil guys who wants to like, fly us to Dubai or something and make us his live-in sex slaves for a month?"

I have her a look of incredulity. "I seriously doubt it. Probably just someone from the security team who wants to scare us about sneaking into the club. After all, legally we're not supposed to be here."

"That'd be boring."

"We will be lucky if boring is the only thing that happens tonight."

"I can assure you – nothing boring ever happens at Cherry Lane."

The voice didn't belong to Laura or the guard.

It was rich and deep and honeyed, the voice of someone who could intimidate and charm you all at the same time.

I spun around slowly, the club swirling all around me as if I were in the middle of a surreal dream, the massive cherries over the DJ booth a red blur.

Holy fuck. The man who stood before me was easily the most handsome man I'd ever seen.

He was nearly six and a half feet tall. His dark hair, the color of melted chocolate, was short and slicked back, long enough to tuck behind his ears. His eyes were dark, narrowed slightly in a manner where I couldn't quite tell if he were amused or annoyed at the sight of me.

His nose was slim, but curved just a bit to the side, as if it'd been broken and reset. His lips were full and wide, the faintest hint of a smirk on them. The only imperfection on his face, a small, curving scar that started at the edge of his sharp jawline and ended in the middle of his prominent cheekbone.

The things I would let him do to me.

He was dressed in a dark suit clearly tailored for his powerful body. He was confident and self-assured though I couldn't quite make out how old he was.

The sight of him caused me to pull in a sharp gasp of air. My heart began to race, and my pussy clenched. I was a perfect blend of intimidated and turned on.

"Do you work here?" Laura asked. "Because we could really use something to drink." Her tone was bossy, challenging almost.

I wanted to whisper to her, tell her to cool it, but I was so wrapped up in this strange man in front of me that I couldn't even begin to form the words.

"Ah, where are my manners?" he asked himself.

He turned, nodding to one of the nearby waitresses, who eagerly hurried over and awaited his command. "A bottle of our finest mineral water – three glasses."

"Of course, Mr. Nichols."

She sashayed off, her ass perfectly swaying as she made her way to the bar. The flash of electricity in her eyes had made it clear that she would've done anything this Mr. Nichols asked of her.

"Wait, *mineral water?*" Laura asked. "I was hoping for something a little stronger than that."

I finally had enough of my bearings to lean over and whisper sharply. She only shrugged.

"In normal circumstances, I'd be more than happy to offer a pair of lovely young women something with a little more punch to drink. But considering you two are both underage..."

My heart jumped into my throat. He knew, and more than likely, came over to throw us out, possibly blacklist us from Cherry Lane for good.

The waitress returned, setting the three glasses on the table before cracking open the bottle and pouring a little bit for each of us.

"How did you know we were underage?" I asked, realizing right away how silly of a question it was.

He chuckled as he slid into the booth next to me. His nearness was almost too much to take, electricity sparking between us. I could sense that he knew what he was doing, knew that he had this hold on me.

"I could tell you were underage because I've been doing this a long time and I've got good instincts."

He looked from Laura to me. As those dark, hunter's eyes landed on mine, it felt as if he were looking straight through me, right into my very soul. "I'd guess twenty – both of you. Though likely closer to twenty-one."

"She's only a few months away from twenty-one," Laura said.

He turned toward Laura and said, "Only a few months away is still under twenty-one. And while this is an exclusive club, I *do* strive to obey the law."

Despite his words, I got the distinct impression that he'd likely break any law if it were beneficial to him.

He leaned forward, clasping his hands together. I glanced down at them, noticing how rough they were, how calloused.

"You're security, right?" I asked.

The slight, amused smile still on his face, he slowly turned his gaze to me.

Every move he made was precise and deliberate. A further sign of his confidence. "What makes you say that?"

I nodded to his hands. "The callouses."

He arched his eyebrows, intrigued. "Oh?"

"Those knuckles are the kind you get when you, well, use them a lot."

"Very perceptive. And yes – security is part of my job here at Cherry Lane. So, that's one question for you. Now's my turn. Why are you both here?"

"For fun!" Laura piped up. "What other reason would there be?"

Mr. Nichols narrowed his eyes and leaned forward.

He wasn't amused by Laura's blithe attitude.

"Listen, ladies – while you're here, as far as I'm concerned, you're trespassing. Now, this is your one warning not to bullshit me. Got it?"

As he spoke, something occurred to me.

He was perfect.

Not just in terms of how damn good-looking he was but in terms of the job I needed him to do.

He was tall and strong and intimidating, as well as smooth and professional.

He was exactly the kind of man I needed.

"OK, here's why we're here," I began.

I took a deep breath, knowing it was time to put it all on the table.

"We're here to find someone like you."

CHAPTER 4

JACOB

Her words were enough to distract me, if only for a moment, from how stunning she was.

The girl was so damn beautiful that it took all the self-control I had to retain my composure. The notion was more than a little unsettling to me.

I was the sort of man for whom self-control came naturally – especially when it came to women.

With her wavy, honey-brown hair, her wide, expressive blue eyes, her full, plush lips, not to mention what had to have been about the best damn body I'd ever seen, the girl before me awakened feelings and urges that I'd thought were long dormant.

It took me a moment to push them aside, to focus on the very strange thing she'd just said.

"You're here for someone like me?"

She pursed her lips, as if trying to decide whether to press forward or to take it all back. Then she took in another full breath that pushed her breasts forward - it took all my restraint not to stare at the beautiful mounds peeking out of the low-cut dress she wore.

"I need someone," she said. "Someone who's strong and knows how to handle themselves."

"For what? I should let you know now that I'm not a hitman."

Although that wasn't entirely true, I didn't need to get into all that.

"Delilah's mom," her friend said, jumping in. "She wants to take over and manage all of her money, her trust fund."

Delilah – so that was her name.

How fitting.

I raised my palm. "Ladies, whatever this is about, why don't we go to my office to discuss it further?"

"Your office?" Delilah asked.

Her friend leaned forward. "What? Why? This isn't some trick, is it?"

I couldn't help but chuckle. "What kind of a trick?"

Her friend shrugged. "I don't know, drug us and put us into some sex trafficking operation."

"Laura! At least try to be polite!"

"Nothing like that goes on here at Cherry Lane," I assured her. "Every woman here is here because she wants to be. And she can leave at any time. That goes for the two of you, as well."

I could tell that Delilah was thinking it over, wondering if it was time to get up and get the hell out of there. But she didn't. Instead, she squared her shoulders, sat up straight, and spoke.

"Then let's do it. I came here for a man, and I'm not about to leave empty-handed." Her face flushed.

"I mean, that came out wrong. It's..." She closed her eyes and focused. "It's easier if I just tell you what I mean."

This, I had to hear. "Then come. We'll take the elevator up."

I rose, offering my hand to Delilah. She regarded it with a bit of apprehension, but she took it. As our skin made contact, a white-hot heat ran through my body.

The feeling was so intense that I only allowed myself to hold her hand for a moment, letting it go and turning away when she was on her feet.

"Oh, I don't get a hand?" Laura asked cheekily.

Normally, I would've offered but Delilah had distracted me.

"You're a big girl," I replied. "You'll manage. Come."

Laura scoffed, but I paid it no heed. Without another word, we made our way through the first floor to the elevator.

We rode up in silence. Archie was standing just outside the doors as they opened.

"All good, boss?" he asked.

"All good. I'm going to take a meeting. Stay close at hand."

"Got it."

I opened the door as the four of us reached my office at the far end of the hall, holding it for Delilah and Laura.

Archie entered behind me, taking his usual post during meetings.

I could tell right away that my office wasn't what the girls had expected. The space was decorated in rich, dark wood, with leather wingback chairs in front of my grand, oak desk. Three windows to the left looked down onto the club, and prominently displayed behind where I sat were the Olympic medals I'd won during my days as a boxer.

"This is your office?" Delilah asked.

"It is. Welcome."

Her eyes flicked up to the medals. "Wait, are those yours?"

"They better be," I said. "I took enough punches to earn them."

It was Laura's turn to speak. "Wait – so you're the *boss* of this place?"

I grinned. "That's right. Cherry Lane is mine."

"But you said you were security," Delilah reminded me.

"He is," Archie chimed in. "Among other things."

"Security, HR, booking – nothing happens here without my knowing. You ladies really didn't research this place before you arrived, did you?"

"Not like we could go on Google and find out about it," Laura said. "Believe me, I tried after the last time I was here."

I gestured for the girls to sit down. They did, and I took my place behind my desk.

"Now," I said. "Tell me again the reason you two came here. You wanted to find a man?"

Delilah pursed her lips. "That's right. It's a weird situation, but I can tell you if you're interested. I'm sure you won't want to do it, but maybe one of the guys who works for you will."

As she spoke, all I could think of was how much I wanted her. I wished that she and I were alone, that I could hike up that dress of hers, pull down her panties and take her over my desk. My cock was half-hard as I sat there.

I couldn't remember the last time I'd felt this way about a woman. "Go on."

She took a deep breath, then continued. Delilah spun me a tale of a massive inheritance and a mother who wanted to get her hands on it.

It was almost too strange to process, but as she spoke, I began to develop the impression that she wasn't the lying sort.

No, she was too innocent for that. Not to mention, what could she possibly hope to gain from lying?

"So," I said when she'd finished her story, "you want a tough guy to pretend to be your fiancé. You want a man who can look your mother in the eye and tell her that the money is all yours, that you're starting a new family and she needs to back off."

"I know it sounds silly," she said. "But my mom is a master manipulator and I'm sick of her bullshit. I just want another line of defense, so she won't even try. Fighting with her is exhausting."

She sighed and I could see that exhaustion plain on her face. "Let me ask you this," I said. "What are you prepared to offer a potential client to take on this role?"

"I have a couple thousand in savings. I was hoping that'd be enough to work as a deposit. Once I turn twenty-one, I'll have access to the rest of my money."

"Twenty-five thousand," Laura interrupted. "That's how much she's going to offer in total."

"What?" Delilah spun her head towards Laura, shocked.

"You need a nice, round number. And I know how much you're going to get – this is nothing compared to what your mom would try to take from you."

Delilah pursed her lips once more. Then she nodded.

"Twenty-five thousand dollars."

I leaned back in my seat, folding my hands over my lap.

"And the job would require, what, exactly?"

"A few meetings with my mom, maybe some FaceTime calls. Just enough to convince her that we're the real deal and that she needs to back off. Once I have the money, I'm going to start looking into places to invest it. That way when I 'call the engagement off,' the money's going to be safely tucked away where she can't even try to get at it."

I glanced away, thinking the matter over.

"Well?" Laura asked. "You've got to have at least *one* guy here who would do it. Twenty-five thousand's a lot of money."

Delilah said nothing, instead regarding me with those big, innocent eyes of hers, as if silently pleading with me.

Right then, I knew exactly what I wanted.

"Alright," I said. "I'll do it."

Neither of the girls knew quite what to say. They looked at one another, then at me.

"What?" Delilah asked. "*You'll* do it?"

"Are you joking?" Laura followed up.

"I'll do it." I glanced back to see that even Archie was stunned by what I'd said. "You need a man to do this job – I'll do it."

Laura closed her eyes and held her palms up, as if she needed a moment to compose herself.

"Now, don't get me wrong – that's awesome! But why do you

want to do it? You're the boss of this place, right? Don't you have, well, bigger things to worry about?"

"Perhaps. But I've got a good team underneath me – this place would be more than well taken care of if my attention was elsewhere for a bit. You're offering twenty-five thousand, right? That's no small amount of money, and a good price for the work that you need done. Plus, I wouldn't trust anyone else to do it the way I would."

I wouldn't trust anyone else to be in the same room with her and not try to put the moves on her. Not on my watch.

The girls were still stunned. Delilah, however, managed to get her bearings and speak up.

"Great!" She sprang out of her seat so quickly that her breasts shook. It took quite a bit of effort not to stare. She stuck out her hand.

I chuckled, amused.

"What? This is what we do, right? We shake?"

I rose slowly. "We can shake."

I reached out and took her hand. Her skin was so soft, her fingers so slender. It was impossible not to imagine other things she might be able to do with her touch.

"Now what?" Laura asked.

I opened one of my desk drawers and slipped out a pair of business cards.

"I know these are a little old-fashioned," I said. "But I still use them. Keep one, write down your information on the other. Number, address, place of work, everything."

Archie approached Delilah and held a pen out in front of her before she even had a chance to ask. She flicked those big eyes up at me one more time before placing the card on the desk and jotting down her information. Then she passed it over.

"Excellent. I'll be in touch."

"I need something more definite than that," she said. "There's a dinner at my mom's house on Sunday – I'd need you there for that."

"Noted," I said. I looked over at Archie. "Escort them out, make sure they're on their way safely."

"You got it, boss."

I smiled at Delilah. "Looking forward to working together."

Without another word, I gestured to the door. Delilah and Laura both regarded me with suspicion before following Archie out.

Once I was alone, I allowed myself a moment to calm down.

It had been difficult to be around her – that was something I had not been prepared for. After pouring myself a drink from my private bar, I stepped over to the windows and looked down at the club below.

It didn't take long to spot Delilah. Even among the large crowd, a woman like her stood out. I yearned for her, wanted her so badly that it hurt.

I knew I'd have my chance.

I sipped and watched as Delilah and Laura left the club. Fifteen or so minutes later, a knock sounded at my door.

"Come in."

Archie entered, closing the door behind him. I gestured for him to make himself a drink.

"OK," he said. "You're the boss. And one of the lessons I've learned since starting here is that you know what you're doing – even if it doesn't sound like it at the time."

"But..."

"But I gotta ask – what the hell is this all about?"

Archie was quite possibly the only man on the planet I'd let question me like that. I liked it that way – I needed someone with a good head on his shoulders who wasn't afraid to tell me what he really thought. Sometimes I needed to be checked.

"Because" he went on, "I know it's not about helping that girl out. And I *damn* well know it's not about the twenty-five thousand dollars. Jesus, Mary, and Joseph – you've likely made twenty-five thousand dollars in the time it took for me to see the girls out."

He was probably right about that.

"I'll tell you what it's about, Arch. It's about the girl."

"Yeah, I figured as much. But why her? You can have your pick from any of the girls down there on the dance floor. Delilah is ridiculously gorgeous, sure, but there's got to be another woman out there just like her."

I turned and gazed once again at the club below me.

"No. She's got something that none of those women down there have. She's innocent. I'm going to take her. And I'm going to make her mine."

CHAPTER 5

DELILAH

It was Sunday afternoon, the day of my dinner with Mom.

And I was sure that I'd gotten ghosted by Jacob.

"You have his business card, right?" I was in the break room of Culprit Coffee, the shop near campus where I worked as a barista. A panini that I'd bought for lunch was in front of me, but I was too tense to take a bite. Instead, I was doing a FaceTime call with Laura.

"Yeah." I reached into my purse and slipped out the card. "But the only thing on it is his name."

Laura sighed. "Well that sucks. What're you going to do if you don't hear back from him?"

"I mean, what *can* I do? I'm going to go to dinner at Mom's and deal with her bullshit as usual." My stomach tightened at the mere thought.

The only reason I was going was to see my sisters and show them some solidarity. My younger sister was still under thumb, and I wanted her to know I wouldn't abandon her.

If it weren't for them, I'd have been done with my mother's dinners a long time ago.

"You have to try something. Oh! What about going back to the club and seeing if Jacob's there?"

"You make it sound so simple. You remember how hard it was to get in there before. Not a chance we manage it a second time. Nope – if he doesn't want to do it, then that's the end of it."

A knock sounded at the break room door. Megan, the manager on duty, poked her pretty, cheerful face inside.

"Hey, I know you're on your break, but Sean and I are slammed up front. Any chance I can get you to clock back in? I'll let you go a little early tonight if you do."

"Sure!" I turned to Laura. "You heard her – time to get back to it."

"Alright. Good luck tonight. And if you need a pep talk before the dinner, you know you can call me."

"I know. Love you."

"You too."

We hung up and I sprang out of my seat, dropping the panini into the trash and grabbing my apron off the door as I went out onto the main floor with Megan.

Sean smiled at me in the broad, happy way he always did when he saw me. The placidity of his face was a funny contrast to the bustling crowds of people behind him, as if seeing me was enough to put him in a dreamy daze.

"Hey, Des," he said, raising his hand and giving me a waggly finger wave. "How was your break?"

I hurried to his side in front of the four-spout espresso machine and scanned the order tickets. There was plenty to do, but nothing I couldn't make with my eyes closed and one hand behind my back.

"Break was fine, thanks," I answered as I worked.

"Those are cool shoes," Sean said.

"Huh?" I glanced down at the white low-top Chuck Taylors I happened to be wearing. "Oh, thanks."

The grinding of beans for espresso shots, the hiss of steam for frothing milk, and the chatter of the customers drowned out all other conversation.

For a few moments anyway.

"So, you got any plans tonight after work?"

Sean was sweet and nice, and he also had a pretty big crush on me. On paper, there was nothing wrong with the guy.

Try as I might, however, I couldn't summon up my feelings to match his.

It wasn't just Sean, however. I'd never felt a specific connection with any guy. Which was precisely why I was still a virgin.

In fact, the only guy that had ever made me feel any spark of electricity that I'd want to give any of my valuable time to was Jacob.

"Um, dinner with my mom. Boring stuff."

"Oh." Disappointment shadowed his face. Sean always took it hard whenever I turned him down.

"I was going to see if you wanted to go get sushi or something."

"Maybe some other time."

"Hey Delilah, can I get a caramel frap, extra caramel?" Megan called out.

"On it!"

I was thankful for the task as it ended the awkward moment with my coworker.

The hours flew by, and by the time the rush was over it was nearly time for my shift to end. I checked my phone one last time to see if Jacob had texted - he hadn't - before hanging up my apron and clocking out.

I made myself a latte, so I had something to sip on for the drive back to my apartment. Dinner was at six, which meant I had three hours to mentally prepare myself for the nonsense ahead.

Instead of leaving right away, I sat out on the back patio and sipped my coffee, taking in the mellow late afternoon air and trying to pretend, at least for a while, that I didn't have a care in the world. I lived just off campus, which meant that I didn't need to hurry to get home.

I finished my coffee and stood to go. One last check of my phone revealed that Jacob hadn't messaged me – and at this point there was no reason to believe he would.

"Hey, Des?"

Sean's voice snapped me out of my daydreaming.

"What's up?"

"There's...a guy out front. He wants to talk to you."

"What, like a pissed off customer or something?"

"No, not like that. But he said he wants to see you."

With that, he turned and went back inside. I picked up my empty cup and dropped it in the trash on the way in. As soon as I was back in the café, I saw Jacob standing on the sidewalk through the glass front of the store.

"Who's *he*?" Megan asked, her eyes wide and locked onto Jacob.

"Just this guy I know. Um, see you later."

The man looked *good* in a white Henley, dark jeans, and a pair of black boots. He wore the casual look as well as he had his tailored suit.

He leaned against what had to be the nicest sports car I'd ever seen in my life, the color a deep, blood red. His eyes were hidden behind aviator sunglasses, his hair slicked back and a small smirk on his gorgeous face.

"There you are," he said, his voice as low and sensual as I'd remembered it. "Ready to ride?"

CHAPTER 6

JACOB

It'd taken some serious restraint not to pounce on her right then and there.

Delilah might have been dressed in a simple, casual outfit of jeans, sneakers, T-shirt, and visor for the coffee shop, but with a body like hers she didn't need anything more than that to get my head filled with visions of her naked and writhing underneath me.

"Hey." She said the word softly.

I could sense that my unannounced visit at her place of work had been the last thing she'd expected.

Surprising her had been half the fun.

She approached me, looking me up and down with those innocent, blue eyes of hers.

"I'm not a mirage," I said. "You can even touch me, if you want."

And I definitely *did* want her to touch me.

"I'll take your word for it." She smiled slightly, her reaction to seeing me guarded and measured. "Why are you here?"

"Why do you think I'm here? You have a dinner tonight, right?"

She seemed unsure. "You still want to do that?"

"Didn't drive all the way out here for nothing."

"A little notice would've been nice. I felt pretty sure when I didn't hear from you that I was never going to see you again."

"I'm here now. Let's go."

Her eyes flashed, and I could sense that part of her had been expecting me to be more apologetic but groveling for forgiveness wasn't my style.

Instead, I opened the door for her and stepped aside. She let out a frustrated sigh, then slipped into the car as I shut the door behind her.

Seconds later, I was in the driver's seat.

"Where do you live?"

"Kelton and Levering. Just a few minutes away. I usually just walk."

I started the car, gunning the engine of my Bugatti, grabbing the attention of everyone around the way my ride always did.

Having her near me again was more intense than I'd expected it to be.

The wind blew through her honey-brown hair, her blue eyes searching around as she bit her lower lip in uncertainty.

I wanted her like crazy, wanted to pull the car over, throw her into the backseat, and fuck her the way I'd been fantasizing about since I'd last seen her.

I held back. After all, I had plans for Delilah. Making my move right then and there would've ruined them.

We drove on, the coffee shop only a short distance from her apartment.

"Where's your car?" I asked.

"I don't have one."

"Living in LA without a car. That's bold."

"Well, it's less about boldness and more about not having the money. I'm a broke as hell student in case you forgot."

"Right. But you're a broke as hell student temporarily."

She nodded. "Yeah. Don't remind me."

I chuckled. It wasn't long before she pointed out her apartment, one of those standard two-story buildings with hacienda stylings and stucco walls that you saw all over LA in mid-range neighborhoods.

We parked and I made sure to get out before her to open the door.

She smiled softly as she stepped out of the car, and I could sense she wasn't used to men opening doors for her.

"Thanks." She glanced behind her. "This is me. You don't have to come in if you don't want to. My place is kind of a mess."

"I'd love to come in."

She nodded and tucked her hair behind her ear. "I won't be long – just need to change."

I gestured forward. "After you."

Delilah flicked those blue eyes on me once more, and they were even more brilliant in the late afternoon sun. Turning with a small smile, she started toward her building.

I followed her, taking in the sight of the place.

"It's not much," she said as we approached the door, and she slipped her keys out of her purse. "Probably nothing compared to what you're used to."

She was right and wrong.

"These days, maybe," I replied as she opened the door. "But I lived in more than a few places like this when I was younger."

Delilah glanced over her shoulder at me, and I could sense that my comment had made her, if only for a moment, keenly aware of the age difference between us.

When I was her age, she'd been in elementary school.

She opened the door and we stepped into a small, but cozy space, brightened up with fresh flowers, colorful furniture, and cheerful art.

"Can I get you anything?" she asked as she let her purse slide off her arm onto the bar that separated the living area from the kitchen.

"Water's fine."

With one more smile, she stepped over to the fridge and opened it. Delilah bent over to reach inside, and my eyes immediately went right to her perfect, heart-shaped ass.

Her body was flawless, phenomenal. I was ogling her like a horny teenage boy.

She turned with a bottle of water in each hand, stepping over to me after shutting the fridge with a quick bump of her hip.

"Thank you."

"Of course. You can have a seat here." She glanced down as she spoke, pausing when she realized that her couch was covered in clothes and school material.

She hurriedly moved things around to give me a place to sit.

"I won't be long – I'm just going to change out of my work clothes."

"Take your time, I'll keep myself busy."

She glanced at the TV. "I've got Netflix if you want to watch anything."

Delilah hurried out of the room, and I eased into the seat, chuckling a bit to myself as she left. I looked around, noting the décor – all sketches of various marine animals.

A glance down at her notes strewn on the coffee table revealed more of the same. I picked one up, a sketch of a seahorse that had been done with scientific precision, reminding me of naturalist sketches done by scientists over a century ago.

Impressive.

Suddenly, a thud sounded out, followed by an "Ow, *shoot!*"

I glanced over. To my surprise, the bedroom door had been left open a good foot or two. It was more than enough to see inside.

Delilah was there with her foot in her hands and a pinch of pain on her face.

She had nothing on but a skimpy pair of white panties and a black bra. Her body was stunning, just as I'd expected, with round hips, a sculpted ass, and a pair of perfect tits that seemed on the verge of bursting out of her bra.

Her stomach was flat and toned, her legs flawless.

My cock went hard at the sight of her.

I wasn't the peeping tom sort, but I let my eyes linger on her for a second longer, then using all the will I had to pull my attention away from her.

My cock was stone solid from merely the fleeting glimpse of Delilah in her underwear. My mind flashed back to the other night, when I'd met her in my office and been so turned on that later I'd managed to make myself come to the lingering scent of her in the room.

I let my mind wander, imagining what it'd be like to get up and walk into her room.

I could picture the shocked expression she'd likely have on her face as I stepped into her bedroom, her breasts rising and falling slowly as her breath quickened.

I'd step over to her, place my hands on her hips and feel the soft, warm flesh of her curves.

Then, I'd lean in and kiss her, Delilah's body going stiff at first, then relaxing as I opened my mouth and let my tongue meet hers.

She'd be surprised, but her tension would release more and more as she lost herself in the kiss. She'd place her hands on my broad shoulders and kiss me back hard, moving her body against my erection and pressing into it, asking for it without saying a word.

I'd take off her bra, letting her ample, round breasts tumble out and into my hands.

"You like when I touch you like that?" I'd ask, my fingers teasing her nipples as they grew harder by the second.

The pleasure would be so intense, so unexpected, that all she'd be able to do is look at me with those big, blue eyes and nod.

I'd knead her perfect tits for a few moments longer before taking my right hand and placing it between her soft, warm thighs, pressing my fingertip against her clit through her soaking wet panties.

She'd moan and buck into me, grinding hard and yearning for more. When I'd brought her to the edge, I'd lean in close and whisper.

"Tell me what you want."

She'd be too turned on, too focused on the orgasm that was on the verge of breaking loose. She'd be putty in my hands.

"I want you to fuck me."

Just what I'd want to hear. I'd take my hand away and hook my thumbs underneath her panties, pulling them down past her thighs and exposing her glistening pussy.

She'd do the same to me, opening my pants and wrapping her slender fingers around my thick, throbbing cock. I'd put my hands on her hips once more, turn her around and push her up against the wall, her round ass bent over for me.

I'd place my head at her opening, sharp gasps escaping her mouth as I prepared to push. Then, with one full, hard thrust, I'd—

"Sorry that took so long."

My eyes flashed as I took in the sight of her. She was dressed in a pair of black jeans, an off-white blouse, and dark red flats – nice, but casual. "It's impossible to keep track of anything in there."

Noticing the look on my face, she cocked her head to the side. "You OK?"

I gave myself a moment to come back to reality. I'd gotten so lost in the fantasy that it took effort to realize that she was in front of me fully clothed, not bent over and naked.

"I'm OK. Let's go."

I had a feeling it was going to be a very interesting night.

CHAPTER 7

DELILAH

Jacob opened the passenger side door to his car as we approached, and I slid into the smooth leather seat of his sports car. Seconds later, he was behind the wheel and turning over the powerful engine.

I reached into my purse and pulled out a stack of hundreds that I'd picked up from the bank in the event he had wanted to work with me.

"Here."

Jacob glanced at me; his brow knitted in confusion above the ink-dark squares of his sunglasses.

"What is that?" he asked.

"The money?" I answered, holding the stack out. "You know, the money I agreed to pay you to do this?"

The confusion vanished and he nodded.

"Right. Open the glovebox and stick it in there. No need for you to be walking around with that kind of money on your person."

I did as he asked, opening the glovebox in front of me and putting the money inside.

"So," he said as he turned onto Wilshire. "Where are we headed?"

"My mom's place, or Sam's place, is in Brentwood Heights. For now, just take Wilshire to Bundy and then head north."

"Got it. So, who's Sam?"

"He's my mom's newest guy."

"Must do pretty well for himself if he's in Brentwood Heights."

"Yeah, he does. But he's also the most boring man I've ever met in my life. He's the owner of a chain of laundromats, and I swear, the only time you can get the blank expression off his face is by mentioning profit margins or stuff like that."

"But your mom likes him just fine."

"The fact that he's worth seven figures is more important to my mom than anything interesting he could have to say."

"Ah. So, we've got two common LA types – the money obsessed man who's a blank void outside of his work, and the gold-digging woman eager to sink her claws into him."

"You've got it."

Jacob didn't mince words. Part of me was shocked at how easily he'd been able to size up the situation. He was cynical and well-traveled enough to understand.

"And I'm going to guess that he's not the first guy your mom has sized up in this way?"

"Nope. But he's definitely the biggest catch. Mom's been working on her game for a while. When my sisters and I were kids, she was running around with guys who owned bars or whatever. But she's had her eyes on the prize for a while, always ready to trade in the guy she was with for one a little further up the ladder. I guess Sam's the one she's decided on, with getting pregnant and all."

He arched one of his thick, dark eyebrows. "She's pregnant?"

"Was. Six months ago, she had my youngest sister."

He chuckled, seeming to find it all wryly amusing.

"That's got to be weird," he said. "Having a sibling twenty years younger than you."

"Weird doesn't even begin to describe it." A thought occurred to me. "What about you? You have any brothers or sisters?"

His response was swift and sudden, and, with a single utterance, he said what I knew would be all there was to say on the issue.

"No."

The word hung in the air, and I shifted in my seat nervously, feeling like I'd crossed a line.

"But you do," he said. "What other family will be there?"

If he was upset by my question, he didn't show it.

"My other two sisters – Maryann, my older sister, and Corrine, who's younger than me. Neither of them have families of their own yet. They'll be there tonight."

"Nice little family dinner," he said. "And do they know I'm coming?"

"Why would they? I didn't even know you were coming until you showed up at my work."

I directed him to make a turn and he followed.

Before too long, we arrived at Sam and Mom's place. The home was a standard Brentwood affair, a vaguely southwestern style, three-story home hidden behind one of the tall, rectangular shrubs in the area that were often used to block the view of houses from the roads.

We pulled into the driveway, right next to Sam's bright yellow Porsche. Jacob let out an amused snort as he looked over at the car.

"Not your style?"

"If you hadn't told me that this Sam guy was new to money and wanted to show it off, this car would've said it just as well."

I didn't know enough about fancy cars to understand the messages sent by each individual model.

What I *did* know was that Porches were expensive. If Jacob was scoffing at one for being a "show off" car, it really made me wonder what kind of money he was worth.

We stepped out of the car and headed toward the front doors. My stomach tightened the closer we got to the entrance.

What kind of person would Jacob be in front of my family? Was he going to roll his eyes at Sam, dress down my mom, hit on my sisters? It dawned on me just then how little I had thought this through.

Was I about to fuck this up even worse?

The front door opened as we made our way down the winding, flagstone path through the enormous front lawn. Mom's familiar shape appeared in the door, and her eyes went straight to Jacob.

"Is that the famous Ms. Kline?" Jacob's voice sounded different.

Instead of rough and aggressive, it was warm and inviting. I turned to see him flashing a smile at my mom, the sort of disarming, toothy smile that made me wonder if his true calling was somewhere in Hollywood.

"De-De?" Mom called me by my nickname as she stepped out of the shadows. Lila was in her arms, cute as ever. "Who's this?"

Jacob approached her fearlessly, as if he'd been waiting all his life to meet my mom.

"My name's Jacob Nichols. It's a real pleasure to meet you."

I could tell right away by the look on Mom's face that she was more than happy to meet him, too.

As different as Mom and I might've been in temperament, we were spitting images of one another. We were both tall and curvy with brown hair that made for perfect beach waves.

Mom's eyes were as blue as mine, but always narrowed into scheming slits, as if she were in a constant state of sizing up people where they stood.

I could tell by everything about her look, from her expensive, billowy clothes, to the gold bangles on her wrists, to the major work she'd had done on her face, that she was settling into her new life as a kept woman.

"Mr. Nichols," Mom said, offering out her free hand. "You're certainly a surprise for the evening."

She was so distracted by Jacob, in fact, that she seemed to forget that she had a baby on her hip.

I hurried in, scooping Lila out of her arms, and holding my sister close. Lila had our big blue eyes, but her hair was a curly blonde, like Sam's. Lila smiled and cooed at me, wasting no time trying to grab my nose like she always did.

"My apologies for dropping by unannounced. I'd been planning on coming with Delilah, but I didn't know until just a few hours ago if I'd be able to make it."

"Not a problem at all. But...I suppose I should ask who you are, exactly."

Well, there was no putting it off any longer.

"Jacob and I," I said, trying to work up truly convincing fake enthusiasm. "We're getting married!"

Mom's big blue eyes went wide, her mouth turning into a perfect "O" of surprise.

"You're *what?*"

CHAPTER 8

JACOB

With those three little words, the plan was on – there was no going back.

It didn't matter. I was ready. Hell, this whole thing might even be a little fun.

Not to mention the pot of gold at the end of the rainbow – the gorgeous, naïve girl I couldn't wait to make all mine.

That part of the plan, however, would need to wait. For the moment, I had a family to charm.

"You're getting *married?*" Delilah's mother was flabbergasted.

She followed up her words of surprise by flicking her eyes down to her daughter's ring finger. My gut tightened as I realized the oversight.

"Where's the ring?"

Delilah flashed me a surprised look, one that made it clear she'd forgotten about the little detail of the engagement ring.

"It happened suddenly. One moment I was with your daughter, the two of us on the beach watching the sunset, and the next I realized that I *had* to marry her. There will be a ring, but it's going to take time to make sure we find just the right one."

Her mother glanced over my shoulder, no doubt checking out my car. "And I'm sure you'll be able to afford it."

"Most certainly," I said with a smile.

I had Delilah's mother summed up right away. A woman like her couldn't help herself when coming face-to-face with money.

She'd seen my car, my shoes, and my watch, and understood instantly that I was a man of means. It was the equivalent of an eighteen-year-old boy seeing a gorgeous woman up close in a bikini – keeping it cool went right out the window.

I was ready to use it to my advantage.

Delilah's mother turned her big blue eyes to me, a sly smile on her face.

"But where are my manners," she asked. "My name's Naomi."

"A pleasure."

We shook, her fingertips grazing my palm as we did.

It was almost funny – I hadn't known this woman for more than five minutes and she was already flirting with me. That was fine, of course. It'd certainly make my job all the easier.

"Holy shit!" shouted a woman's voice from inside the house. "You're getting *married?*"

I glanced up over Naomi's shoulder to see a pair of young women step out onto the porch.

One of them was tall and lithe, with a stunning face and dark hair that fell in tresses over her shoulders. The other was on the petite side, but just as good-looking, her hair the same honey brown as Delilah's.

The resemblance between these two women and Delilah was clear, but if there had been any doubt that they were related, the fact that they had the same set of big, blue eyes would've put that right to rest.

Delilah, the baby still curled up in her arms, let out a squeal of excitement as she laid eyes on her sisters. She passed the baby to the taller of the pair, all of them exchanging hugs as they greeted one another.

Then they laid eyes on me.

Neither of the sisters gave me the same sort of ogling as their mother – they seemed more interested in figuring out just who the hell I was.

"You're getting married?" repeated the shorter of the two. "To *him*?"

"No," Delilah said, a playfully sarcastic tone to her voice. "This is just the guy who I hired to pretend to be my fiancé." She was joking, but the flash of surprise on her face made it clear she'd accidentally hit close to home with her crack.

She quickly regained her composure.

"God, I'm being so freaking rude. Everyone, this is Jacob Nichols – my fiancé."

"Extremely pleased to meet you all," I said.

"Jacob, you've already met my mom, Naomi. These are my two sisters. The taller one is Maryann, and the shorter is Corrine."

Corrine rolled her eyes. "You know, there's, like, a million ways you could introduce me other than just calling me 'the shorter one'."

"I've always liked it," Maryann said with a smirk.

Just then someone else joined the group, a middle-aged man with thinning hair, a full beard, and a blue and white striped polo shirt pulled over a big belly. No doubt this was the man of the house.

"Listen, Jacob," he said, coming over to me. "I'm very eager to make your acquaintance and all that. But I have to ask – is that a freaking *Bugatti*?"

I allowed myself a small grin. While I drove the car because I liked it, I couldn't help but be amused at the effect it had on certain types of men, the ones who owned Porches and thought that made them the king of the universe.

"It is," I said. "But I have a little rule – I don't let anyone get close unless we're on a first name basis." I followed this up with a disarming grin, letting him know I was only messing around. He flashed a look, one that seemed to say, "where the hell are my manners?"

"Sam Willard," he said, sticking out his hand. "Pleased as hell to meet you, Jacob." He shook my hand hard in the "alpha male wannabe" sort of way. It was all pretty damn amusing.

"Jacob Nichols."

Sam gave my hand one more squeeze before letting go and gesturing to the house.

"Come on in! Got the big green egg going, there's plenty of BBQ for everyone."

We entered the house, Naomi shutting the door behind me and flashing me another sly look that made it more than clear she was interested. What kind of mother flirted with her own daughter's fiancé?

We stepped into the big, open kitchen where plates of freshly cooked meat and sides were waiting for us. The sight of it was enough to make my stomach growl – I'd had one of those days where I'd been so busy that I'd forgotten to eat.

Sam passed out beers to those who were old enough to drink, and after making our plates we all sat out back at the big table near the pool. The weather was pleasant, and I allowed myself a few moments of relaxation as I sipped my beer and took in the night air.

Delilah was filling them in on how school was going, and Lila sat on her lap as she spoke, the baby looking up at her sister with big, blue eyes.

The sight did something to me, something that I couldn't quite wrap my head around.

As the women caught up, I made sure to chat with Sam a bit. Men like him weren't hard to talk to – all you had to do was ask them about their job and look impressed while they told you how busy they were and how much money they were making.

I got the impression right away that Sam lived to work. It also seemed like he didn't know about Naomi's past, jumping from man to man looking for the next paycheck.

We bonded over the fact that we were both business owners, both men who came from nothing and made something of ourselves.

For a time, the evening seemed like it might be peaceful, easy, even. Then there was a lull in the conversation and Naomi's expression turned serious.

I knew it was about to be the time to step into action.

"You know, De-De," she said. "I realize you're busy with school and all that. But your birthday isn't too far off. And you know what *that* means..." She trailed off.

Naomi didn't need to say exactly what was on her mind but judging by the looks that fell on everyone's face, it was obvious what subject had just been brought up.

I leaned in, ready to listen and enter the conversation when it was time.

"I don't want to talk about this, Mom," Delilah said, her voice sharp. There was silence, only Lila's cooing and giggling breaking it.

"Well, to be frank, it doesn't matter what you want. You're about to come into some serious money here in the near future, and I want to talk about what you're planning on doing with it."

Delilah narrowed her eyes. "We don't need to talk about what I'm doing with it. It's *my* money and that's the end of the story."

Now, I knew my job was to back Delilah up, to make sure her mother didn't have the chance to put the screws to her. However, first I wanted to get a sense of the dynamic.

Naomi's expression turned sad, and she pouted slightly. "Now, it'd be nice if that *were* the end of the story. But it's not."

Confusion flashed on Delilah's face. "What're you talking about, Mom? You've got money. Or, more specifically, *Sam's* got money. Are you really going to sit here and try to get me to open my wallet when we're in the backyard of your Brentwood mansion?"

Naomi glanced over at Sam, the two of them sharing a look that seemed to say that they both had the same thing on their mind, but that neither was quite sure how to say it.

The sisters shared a look of their own. I sipped my beer, wryly amused by the whole unfolding.

"There's more to it than that, sweetie," Naomi said. "We have a lot here, sure. But..."

"We're leveraged to the hilt," Sam said. "Just about everything here's leased. I just did a major expansion for the store and until it gets paid off, *if* it gets paid off, we're one bad month away from selling it all."

"Are you serious?" Delilah asked. "And you've got a *Porsche* out there?"

Sam shrugged. "In the circles I run in, a car like that gets you a long way. It's an investment, of sorts."

I allowed myself a small chuckle – one that no one at the table noticed.

Sam's story was a common one. He found himself a bit of success and was using it to make himself look wealthier than he actually was.

Delilah pursed her lips, and I could see that this new information had made an impression on her – especially with her baby sister seated in her lap.

"That doesn't matter," she said, finding her spine. "The situation that you're in because of your inability to manage money...that's *your* business, not mine."

"But you couldn't be more wrong about that, De-De," Naomi said. "It's not just *us* that you have to worry about, it's Lila."

Maryann cleared her throat and spoke up. "Mom, I don't know if this is the best time to talk about this kind of stuff. We're all here together for the first time in a long while. Maybe we should just enjoy it?"

Naomi scoffed and rolled her eyes. "That's easy for you to say, Maryann. You're not facing the serious financial situation that Sam and I are. I'm well aware that you are unwilling to help out."

I held back, waiting for the perfect moment to jump in.

Delilah sighed, clearly frustrated by the direction the conversation had taken.

"You know what, Mom? Here I was, thinking that we might be

able to have a nice, family dinner and not get into money related matters. Should've known that it would only be a matter of time."

Naomi shrugged, seemingly unbothered in the slightest by what her daughter had just said.

"Well, what do you want me to say? I've got a daughter who's about to come into a large amount of money, and we sure could use some of it. I mean, really – is it *that* hard for you to not be selfish for once in your life, after everything that I've done for you? All I've sacrificed?"

"What exactly have you sacrificed Mom?" Delilah shot back.

"Just a little money," Naomi said, pressing her attack, ignoring Delilah's question. "Barely anything compared to what you're getting. And don't just think of me and Sam – think of your sister."

I cleared my throat and spoke up. "Naomi, I don't want to intrude on a family matter."

"Then don't," Naomi said the words with a snap, surprising even me.

"Although we just met, I'm about to be part of this family. Des and I...we've had some lengthy conversations about the matter of her money."

Naomi regarded me with a hard glare, and I could sense that she was eager to see where I was going with this.

"And as a man who has some experience managing large sums of money, I suggested to her that the worst thing she could do when given access to it would be to start spending it or giving it away. To that end, I put her in touch with one of my best accountants."

"Oh?" Naomi asked.

"That's right," I said. "We're still in the process of going over possibilities for investments and such. But we're in agreement that the bulk of her money should be invested. Isn't that right, baby?"

I reached over and placed my hand on her leg, squeezing it firmly. Despite the pretend nature of it, the sensation of her soft flesh underneath the fabric was enough to make my cock move.

I took my hand away, the feeling of her leg almost too much to bear.

"That's right," Delilah said, flawlessly going along with the lie. "I decided that it'd be best to set aside a little money for essentials so I can focus on school, but otherwise it's best if I just invest it and pretend it's not there."

Naomi's blue eyes flicked from me to Delilah and back again, as if searching for any sign that we were being untruthful.

"You're serious?" Naomi asked. "You're about to come into all of that money and you're just going to...stuff it away?"

"Aside from essentials," I said. "Delilah's also going to pay for her tuition in advance. And as much as she loves walking, I managed to talk her into budgeting for a reasonably priced car. Other than that, she wants to invest it and watch it grow."

Out of the corner of my eye, I could see Maryann and Corrine smile – it was easy to see which side of this conflict they were on.

"You're kidding, right?" Naomi asked, her voice tinged with anger and frustration. "You sat down with some accountant and went over every last dollar and didn't even *think* about what your own family might need? What about your little sister?"

Delilah sat up straight and prepared to speak. The discomfort she seemed to feel moments before was gone.

"If any emergencies come up with Lila that need to be paid for, we can discuss them then. But for now, you both are going to have to figure out how to cover everything on your own. She's your child, not mine."

Naomi's mouth formed into a hard line, her eyes still boiling with anger. Sam, on the other hand, simply appeared defeated. Silence fell, and I watched as Delilah went back to her food.

"Now that this is all taken care of," she said. "Why don't we eat? Don't want this food getting cold, now do we?"

I did my best to hide a very pleased smile.

~

The rest of the dinner went without incident. For the time being, Naomi and Sam seemed to have backed off. We left shortly after the meal, Naomi wanting to get home to do a bit of studying before the night was over.

"Thanks," she said. "That was exactly what I'd been hoping for."

"Of course," I said as I drove. "But from where I was sitting, it seemed like you were doing most of the work."

She nodded. "Yeah. It felt good to stand up for myself and put her in her place. I hate it when she tries to use Lila though. I don't want my baby sister to suffer for her parents' poor choices."

"That's because you've got a good heart. And your mother knows how to take advantage of it."

"I suppose so," she said. "Even though I'm used to it, it's still disheartening." She sighed, tucking her hair behind her ear, and looking out onto the city as we drove. "Sorry, I don't mean to complain. Thanks again for tonight."

"My pleasure. Though something tells me that your mother isn't going to give up so easily."

"You're right about that. Not a chance in hell she'll take this news laying down. Not to mention, we're going to need to actually make this look like a convincing engagement."

I pulled to a stop in front of her apartment.

"Let me see you in."

She shook her head. "Oh, no – you don't need to do that."

"I insist."

Without another word, I stepped out of the car and opened her door. She smiled as she stepped out, and, without thinking, I placed my hand on the small of her back to lead her to the apartment.

"Very gentlemanly," she said as we reached the door.

"I have my moments."

We stopped and turned to face one another. The way she looked then, her lips full and wet, her breasts pulling on the fabric of her shirt. I couldn't resist her any longer.

I leaned in and placed my lips on hers, opening my mouth

slightly and finding her tongue with mine. She fell into the kiss, her body going soft against mine as I brought her close enough to feel my hard length against her.

It took me a few moments to come to my senses – if I hadn't, I might've devoured her on the spot.

I put my hands on her hips and gently pushed her away. The look of surprise on her face was priceless.

"Talk to you soon," I said.

She nodded without saying a word, her mouth still open slightly.

I left her with that, a very pleased smile on my face as I walked away.

Despite how satisfied I was with the kiss, a question lingered in my mind.

How much longer could I resist taking what I wanted?

CHAPTER 9

DELILAH

I was left stunned, not able to say a word as I watched Jacob make his way to his car. I was more turned on than I had been in a long time.

I came to my senses, opening the door to my apartment and rushing inside. As soon as I was alone in my place, I wasted no time opening the front button of my jeans and slipping my hand down my panties. I was soaked, Jacob's kiss awakening feelings and desires in me that I didn't even know I had.

I moved over to the couch, laying back as I touched myself. I closed my eyes, imagining him on top of me, imagining his big, powerful body pushing into me with deep, full thrusts, his muscles tensing and releasing.

It was enough to bring myself to orgasm again and again. When I was done, my body spent, a thought occurred to me - there was no way I'd be satisfied until I had the real thing.

It wasn't until the following Wednesday that I heard from him again.

As I was walking home from work, I spotted a sleek black luxury sedan in front of my apartment. As I approached, a suited driver stepped out of the car, his eyes hidden behind mirrored sunglasses despite the sunset.

"Delilah?" he asked, his voice low and commanding.

"That's me."

He nodded. "Mr. Nichols sent me. I'm to bring you to him."

"For what?"

"Those are my orders."

A thrill ran through me.

"Let me run inside and change."

Another nod, and I hurried past him and into my apartment. My heart raced; my stomach tight with anticipation.

All the same, as I stripped out of my work clothes and changed, I made a mental note. When I saw him, I'd make sure to let him know that I wasn't at his beck and call.

If he wanted to see me, he'd need to get in touch with me in advance. There'd be no showing up at my work unannounced, no sending cars and expecting me to eagerly hop inside.

I had work and school, and there was absolutely no time in my busy schedule for last minute impositions. I'd have to look him right in those deep dark eyes and make that clear.

I gulped hard at the mere thought of it. It'd have to be done, and it'd have to be done that night.

I threw on a summer dress that went all the way down to my ankles and didn't show off much of my body.

I didn't want him thinking I was coming over with expectations.

When I was ready, I grabbed my phone and purse and hurried out of my apartment. The driver was still waiting for me at the car. He opened the back door for me, and I slid inside.

The luxury of the car's interior washed over me, the back area soft and plush and surprisingly spacious. A partition was up between the front and the back, and a small bar was illuminated with soft lighting.

I wasn't much of a drinker, but something to calm my nerves sounded nice. I pushed the urge aside, however, not wanting to have my senses dulled in a way that could prevent me from telling Jacob what I needed to.

Instead of alcohol, I took a bottle of sparkling water and cracked it open, watching the city pass me by as we drove out of the UCLA area and north toward Hollywood. I knew where we were going, and by the time we came to a stop in front of Cherry Lane, I was eager to speak to Jacob.

The driver let me out of the car, and right away a pair of security guards stepped out to escort me. Moments later, we were back in that same hall I'd walked with Laura, the tension in my belly building the same way it had the first time.

However, this time, there was no pulsing music as we approached the door. It was still early in the evening, and from the sound of it, the place wasn't hopping quite yet.

Sure enough, when the guards opened the doors, they revealed a much different environment than I'd seen before.

Plenty of people were in the club, but there was no huge dance party in the middle of the room. Instead, well-dressed men and women sat in the booths, conversing quietly and sipping wine and cocktails. Many seemed to be having meetings. A jazz band on stage played mellow, intricate music – a major contrast to the last time I'd been there.

We stepped inside the elevator and were soon on our way up, the doors opening to reveal the fourth floor of the club.

It was hard for me to sort out my feelings as we made our way toward Jacob's office.

I was anxious, excited, and a bit annoyed.

When we reached Jacob's office, one of the men lightly tapped his knuckles on the door.

"Come in," Jacob's low, deep voice sounded.

He was seated at his desk, a glass of what appeared to be whiskey close at hand. The guard with the shaved head, the one who seemed to be Jacob's right hand, was seated in a nearby chair.

A wolfish smile formed on his lips as he laid eyes on me.

"Archie, we'll finish this later."

"You got it, boss."

Jacob nodded to the guards.

"Gentlemen."

The other two men left, shutting the door behind them, and just like that, Jacob and I were alone.

Jacob sat there like a master of the universe, the look on his face indicating he had me right where he wanted me.

The tension built in my body, my pussy clenching.

I cleared my throat and spoke.

"Listen. It's fine *this* time that you called for me like this. But it's not going to happen again. I've got a busy life, and right now my education is the center of it. I can't just drop everything I'm doing and show up whenever you want. Got it?"

He sat in amused silence for a moment before speaking. "Fine."

That was it. Not another word followed.

"Fine?"

"Fine. You made a perfectly reasonable request."

I wasn't sure what I'd expected. Maybe I'd gotten so used to being around immature, entitled college guys that I'd assumed he would flip out over being told what to do.

"Good. I'm glad you're hearing me."

"What else would you expect?"

"I don't know. Something less...calm."

He chuckled, clearly amused by my words.

"I can assure you that losing my cool isn't my style. You don't get very far in my line of work without being able to keep an even temperament."

"Well, I'm glad to hear it. But that still doesn't tell me why you wanted me here to begin with."

He gestured to the couch at the other side of the room.

I lowered myself onto the soft and comfortable leather.

Jacob rose from his desk and made his way over, no hurry to his steps. As he sat down next to me, goosebumps broke out across my skin, and my breath quickened.

I felt drunk, even though I hadn't had a drop of alcohol.

"You'd like to know what I want from you?" he asked.

"Yes." Getting out even the single word was a challenge. My head swam, my heart raced.

Jacob placed his big hand on my thigh, squeezing it just as he'd done at dinner the other night.

This time, he didn't let go.

"I could tell you," he whispered. "But I'd rather show you."

He moved his other hand to the back of my neck, slipping his fingers into my hair and turning my face toward his. Without another word, he brought his lips to mine and kissed me - hard.

The insistent hunger of his lips against mine was almost too much to take. My eyes went wide for a moment, the exhilaration whipping through me.

I felt tight and wet between my legs as his mouth opened and his tongue searched for mine, moving his hand further up my thigh as the kiss grew more intense.

A moan slipped from my mouth, followed by a sharp intake of air. His hand was so close to right where I wanted it, so very close.

"Tell me what you want," he said. "I need to hear it."

"I don't know," I stammered, immediately feeling foolish.

He chuckled softly.

"I think you do. And you know what else? I've got the feeling you've been thinking about it since our kiss."

God, the man was too cocky for his own good, but he was right.

I squirmed in my seat, the want building between us almost too much to bear.

"Tell me I'm wrong." The way he gazed into my eyes in that moment made the idea of lying seem totally impossible.

"You're not."

The corner of his mouth curled slightly, as if he had me right where he wanted me and knew it.

"Tell me what you want."

"I want *you*."

That was all he needed to hear.

Jacob wrapped his arm around the small of my back and pulled me close enough that I could feel his hardness against my thigh.

He leaned in and kissed me fervently, the sensation of his lips against mine, his tongue curious and teasing, and his hard cock against my leg sent a shudder through my body that nearly shook me to my core.

In those moments I felt helpless in the best way possible, I was putty in his hands to do with whatever he wanted.

My hand fell onto his thigh, inches away from his cock. I wanted to touch him so badly, but I'd never touched a man like that before in my life.

He pulled his lips from mine, and once more I could sense by the smile on his face that he knew exactly what was on my mind.

"Tell me what you want," he murmured against my neck, echoing his earlier words.

"I want to touch you."

"Then do it."

His commanding, deep voice stripped away my hesitation.

"I've never touched a man like that before."

His eyes flashed. No doubt he hadn't expected to hear that.

He glanced aside for a moment, taking in the information I'd just given him.

Instant worry rushed in that he was about to reject me for my lack of experience. He no doubt had his choice of experienced women who knew just how to please a man.

"I want you," he finally said. "I want you badly. But you're under no obligation."

His intent was clear. If I wanted things to end, I could've simply left right then and there. He was giving me an out.

I realized I didn't want one. I answered his statement not with words, but with actions.

I placed my hand on his cock, closing my eyes as I stroked him through his slacks. A sound rose from his chest as he clearly understood what that meant.

He moved in and kissed me hard again as I stroked him, his body flush against mine.

Jacob reached up and took hold of my breasts through my dress, squeezing them gently until my nipples went hard against his touch. I felt woozy again, his touch was like a drug my body craved and couldn't get enough of.

He guided me into a laying position on the couch.

He immediately went to work, gently pushing up the soft fabric of my dress and lifting it over my head. In one swift motion, he tossed it onto the floor and had me down to nothing but my bra and panties.

His eyes moved over me slowly, deliberately, as if he didn't want a single trace of my body to go unappreciated.

I'd never been looked at the way he looked at me in those moments.

His eyes still locked onto mine, he reached around and expertly unhooked my bra, pulling it off my shoulders and tossing it aside.

He was still in his clothes, only his tie removed, and the top button of his shirt opened. Being in nothing but my panties with him still dressed made me feel exposed, but in a way that excited me.

"Now," he said, glancing down at my panties. "Take those off."

His tone was stern, commanding. In that moment I could see why he was the man in charge of Cherry Lane.

Though I'd always considered myself an independent woman, his command excited me. So, I hooked my thumbs under the waistband of my panties and peeled them down my thighs. Once they were at my ankles, I kicked them off.

Judging by the look on his face, Jacob was more than pleased with what he saw. He leaned down and kissed me again, this time his right hand falling between my thighs.

He touched me lightly at first, and I moaned, the slightest pressure of his finger against my clit sending waves of pleasure through me.

I closed my eyes and licked my lips, focusing entirely on his touch, his nearness. Jacob started with slow circles around my most sensitive place before alternating with firm presses. Then he placed his fingers on my lips and spread me open, expertly moving them inside of me.

I was absolutely soaked and by the time his fingers entered me I was so close to an orgasm that there was no sense in holding back.

"Now," he said as he touched me in all the right ways. "I want you to come for me."

I opened my eyes to see him gazing down at me, his expression serious, as if there were no debate on the subject of my climax.

"Come for me," he ordered. "Right now."

His touch and his tone were all that I needed. I relaxed, the orgasm breaking loose and coursing through my body.

I moaned, grinding myself against his touch, allowing the climax to light up every molecule of me.

My legs were still shaking as the climax subsided, and I opened my eyes to see Jacob there watching me with a satisfied gaze.

He grinned that wolfish grin that was starting to have an effect on me like nothing else.

"Spread your legs."

His tone was firm and gentle all at the same time. No man had ever spoken to me like that, and all I wanted to do was give myself over to him.

There was something about the way his eyes savored every bit of my body, that made me feel more beautiful than I ever had in my life.

I wanted him to take me, to make me his.

Jacob began undressing.

He took off his shirt, exposing a flawless, powerful body of perfectly toned muscles, his shoulders round, his pecs square, and his abs shredded. There wasn't a drop of fat on his body, and his slightest movements caused his muscles to tense and flex.

He then moved out of his pants, socks and shoes until he was in nothing but a pair of black boxer briefs, the cuffs of them stretched around the thick muscles of his legs, his cock straining against the fabric.

I couldn't wait any longer.

I grabbed onto his waistband and pulled it down, his enormous cock springing out. He was so big and hard and thick that I couldn't help but let my eyes go wide at the sight of him.

He grinned once more, my reaction seeming to amuse him.

Maybe I was insane to think I could take all of him into me my first time.

However, when Jacob moved over top of me, I knew I was about to find out how I was going to accommodate his size.

"Put me where you want me." He spoke the words in the same commanding tone he'd been using.

Despite the whirl of emotions running through me, I didn't need to think twice about where I wanted him.

I wrapped my fingers around Jacob's length, taking a moment to savor his warm thickness against my skin. I stroked him a bit, letting my fingertips dance over his head and shaft, my thumb teasing his tip, gliding over it with his precum.

The way he growled at my touch signaled that I was on the right track.

I placed his head at my opening. He leaned down, bringing his lips to my neck. He kissed me slowly, his tongue teasing my sensitive skin.

Before he could move inside of me, my eyes flashed with a realization.

"What about protection?" I asked.

"Are you on anything?"

I nodded. "The pill. Been on it since I was a teenager, even though I've never, you know, needed it."

He smiled slightly. "Good. You don't need to worry about me. I stay on top of my health. Plus..." he reached up and grazed my cheek with the back of his hand, "...I'd never do anything to hurt you."

I knew he meant it, and in that moment, I was ready to give myself over to him.

"Now," he said. "Tell me what you want."

"I want you inside of me."

He nodded slowly, another pleased smile forming on his lips.

Jacob pushed into me, and the first inch of his length was enough to cause me to gasp, to make my eyes go wide with shock at how intense it felt.

I writhed underneath him as he stretched me. I was wet and ready, but he was still a lot to take.

He moved slowly, gently, giving my body time to adjust to his size. His last few inches glided into me, and when he was fully sheathed, I felt the initial tension melt away.

In fact, I felt complete.

"How are you?" he spoke in a low voice, his hand on the side of my face, cradling it in a way that put me at ease.

"So...so good."

He kissed me again as he pulled back his hips. When he'd taken himself from me, all I wanted was for him to be back inside. I didn't need to wait long at all. He pushed into me once more and this time he entered with total ease, as if his cock were made for me and me alone.

Jacob soon thrust into me at a steady rhythm, the occasional low, deep grunt sounding from him, the noises reminding me of a caveman in the sexiest way possible.

He covered me with kisses as he moved in and out of me, and it took no time at all for him to bring me to the brink of another orgasm.

He lifted his body up, his cock thrusting in and out as his muscles worked.

"I want to watch you come with me inside of you. Now."

Once more, my pleasure was at his command. I relaxed my body, the insistent pace of his thrusts lulling me into a perfect trance-like state.

I came hard.

It felt as if nothing in the world existed other than Jacob and me and the joining of our bodies. I wrapped my legs around him, keeping him as close as I could. I wanted no distance between us as he kissed me and erupted inside me.

He drained himself into me with a hard grunt, his cock pulsing as he pumped me full of warmth. When we were done, our orgasms fading, he slid his cock out of me and held me close.

CHAPTER 10

JACOB

The way I felt after we'd made love was...surprising.

I'd known there was something different about Delilah from the moment I'd first laid eyes on her. Being there with her, her slender, soft body curled up against mine as we basked in the afterglow of what we'd done...the intensity of my feelings was unexpected.

In fact, it scared me a little, and fear tended not to be a word in my vocabulary.

I needed some time to wrap my head around what I was feeling.

Without a word, I slipped out from under her arm and stood. Delilah's eyes opened slowly; those piercing blues brilliant even in the low light of the room. I could tell that she sensed something was wrong.

She sat up, her full, round breasts magnets for the eyes, but I managed to tear my gaze away as I stepped over to the small fridge in the bar of my office.

"You OK?" she asked.

It hit me as soon as she'd said the words that I was being silly, even a bit selfish.

Delilah had given herself to me in a way that she'd never given herself to a man before in her life, and there I was, getting lost in my own thoughts. I decided that whatever feelings I was experiencing in that moment, would be dealt with at a later time.

I pulled two bottles of San Pellegrino from the fridge, along with a small container of cold grapes.

"I'm fine," I said as I returned to her. "Better than fine."

My words must've done some good, as the tension on her face melted away. I cracked the bottle open and handed it over before taking a small plate from the shelf under the table and putting the grapes on top of it.

My white button-up was draped over the back of the couch, and Delilah took it and put it on before sipping her water.

There was something about the way my shirt looked on her, the billowy white fabric draping all the way down to her bare, silky thighs, that made me want her all over again.

I kept my urges in check as I pulled on my boxer briefs and sat back down.

Delilah reached forward and plucked a grape from the pile. Before she could begin to bring it to her mouth, I slipped it from her fingers and finished the job. Surprise flashed on her face but turned to amusement as I placed the grape on the edge of her bottom lip.

She opened her mouth a bit and I gently pushed the grape inside. Closing her mouth, she wrapped her lips around my finger and teased it with her tongue as I slid it out.

I became hard as hell instantly, my mind racing with thoughts of what else she might be able to do with her lips and tongue.

I pushed my passions aside, not wanting to lose control.

A chime sounded from somewhere in the room.

"Shit." Delilah's face snapped into an expression of panic.

She sprang out of her seat and rushed to her purse where she'd left it on the table near the door. She began rifling through her bag, bending over enough to where the bottom of her ass hung out from beneath my shirt.

"Something wrong?" I asked.

She turned, her phone in her hand as she leaned back against the door. Then, after reading whatever messages were on the screen, she let out a sigh of relief.

"I have a study group tonight that I totally spaced on. But it's not for another hour."

I went for my own phone, ready to send a text to Archie. "Then I'll have the car take you back to your apartment."

"Thanks." She didn't even look at me as she said the word, instead snatching her clothes from the ground and quickly putting them on after tossing my shirt onto the couch. I could tell by the speed and urgency with which she moved that she was dead serious about getting to this study group.

"I meant what I said earlier. This was fun and all, but school's the number one thing for me."

"Of course." I stood and made my way over to her, placing my hands on her arms. "I wouldn't think of standing in the way of that."

Once she realized I was being truthful, that I wasn't simply telling her what she wanted to hear, her shoulders relaxed. A small smile appeared.

"This *was* fun," she said. "I'm glad I came over."

"And I'm glad you did, too." I leaned in and kissed her, letting my lips linger on hers for a long moment.

Opening my eyes, I spotted something on the ground. I bent down and picked up her panties.

"Someone was in a hurry," I said with a grin.

Her eyes flashed with surprise, and she clapped her hands onto her hips, giving me a mysterious smile as if leaving her panties on the floor was no accident.

A knock sounded at my door.

"Ready to take her home, boss," spoke Archie from the other side.

"I'll hang onto these," I said. "Doesn't sound like you've got time to change."

She let out a snort of a laugh. "Fine," she said with a smile and a wink.

One more kiss, and then she was off with a glance over her shoulder.

Once she was gone, I poured myself a finger of whiskey and sat at my desk, a big grin on my face.

A smile took hold as I glanced down at Delilah's panties in my desk drawer.

It'd been two days since our little tryst, but the mere sight of them was enough to bring back the memory of how she felt underneath me, her long legs spread wide open, her glistening pussy waiting for me to plunge my cock into it.

I hadn't spoken to her since, and that was just how I wanted it. My plans with Delilah weren't limited to taking her virginity. No – I had much more in mind for her, and those plans would take time.

My phone buzzed on my desk, and a quick check of the screen was enough to give me pause.

"What the hell?"

The text was from Archie. And it read, *Delilah's mom's here to see you.*

Naomi? What on earth was she doing here?

More importantly, how the hell did she know where I worked?

Though I'd only met Naomi once, I had a damn good feeling she was the sort of woman who didn't give up when you told her to screw off. I picked up my phone and fired off a quick response.

Send her in. But stay close at hand.

He reacted with a thumbs up. Moments later, a knock sounded at the door.

"Come in."

The door opened and, sure enough, there stood Naomi.

She wore a long trench coat, the sash pulled tight. Her hair was done up in thick waves, her face painted with red lipstick and dark mascara. Archie was there with her, and I nodded for her to enter the room.

"So," she said, sauntering in on a pair of dark blue high heels. "This is the famous Cherry Lane."

I wasn't in the mood for any bullshit – I wanted to get right to the point.

"How do you know about this place? And what do you want?"

She pouted in a playful way. "Wow, not even a 'nice to see you?' I'm wounded, Jacob."

"I'd tell you it was nice to see you if that was actually the case. Now, answer my questions."

Without being invited to do so, she dropped into one of the chairs across from my desk, crossing her legs in such a way that I could see they were bare.

No doubt she wanted me to be thinking about what she had on under that trench coat.

"Please," she said, waving a hand through the air, long red finger-nails flashing as she did so. "I've been around the block, Jacob – you don't think I know about Cherry Lane, and about who runs it? This place is legendary, and I knew who you were from the moment you stepped into my house. It makes me wonder what my daughter is doing with a man like you."

"I don't believe that's any of your concern. I'll ask again, what do you want?"

She arched her eyebrows. I was taking a hard tone with her, but it didn't seem to have much of an effect. If anything, she seemed amused.

"I'm here for you."

"What the hell does that mean?"

"I mean...Jacob, you, and my daughter." She shook her head, making a tsk-tsk sound. "When you showed up at my house with her, I couldn't believe what I was seeing. She's got to be half your age, handsome."

"So, that's why you're here? To raise your concerns about the age gap?"

She chuckled. "No, I'm not that much of a prude. But I'd be remiss if I didn't take the chance to come here and, ah, get to know my daughter's fiancé, my future son-in-law, a little better."

"Then get to it. What do you want to know?"

She rose slowly, a sly smile playing on her face.

"Well, we could talk about it, Jacob. But talking's *so* boring. For me, there's one way that I really prefer to get to know a man."

Without another word, she undid the sash of her trench coat and slipped it off her shoulders. The jacket fell to her ankles, revealing a body that was completely bare aside from a matching pair of dark red bra and panties.

I had to admit, Naomi looked good, but I only regarded her with the eye of a man who worked in the industry that I did – there was no temptation in the slightest.

I got the distinct impression that this wasn't the first time Naomi had used her body to get what she wanted.

I raised my palm, signaling that it was time to stop.

"Naomi, I'm engaged to your daughter. And do you really need me to tell you how wildly inappropriate this is?"

"Being inappropriate is one of my specialties." She moved with seductive steps over to my desk, taking a seat on the edge. "Give me a chance, and I'll show you what I mean."

I didn't waste a second before stepping away from the desk, putting as much space as I could between us.

"Put your clothes back on right now." My tone was hard, leaving no question as to whether or not I was joking. "Put them on right now or I'll call security and have you escorted out of here in your underwear."

Her expression turned from surprise to anger.

"Something's going on, Jacob. Something with you and my daughter that I don't like one bit. Make no mistake – I'm going to figure out what it is. In the meantime, I'm going to be keeping my Delilah very, very close."

She bent over to pick up her coat, and as she did, I pressed the small button on the underside of my desk that summoned Archie. He opened the door to my office not three seconds later.

"Archie, please escort Naomi out. And make sure you have a picture of her for the no-entry list." I narrowed my eyes as I looked over to Naomi. "You're about to be a member of a very exclusive club."

She glared at me. "This isn't over, Jake."

Archie approached and took hold of her wrist.

"For tonight," I said. "It is."

With that, Archie escorted her out of the office, and out of my club.

The plan had just gotten a hell of a lot more complicated, but I was even more determined to see it through.

CHAPTER 11

DELILAH

It was Friday, and I was in Santa Monica on the beach, watching the waves as they gently rolled onto the sand and pulled back again.

Santa Monica was my happy place, the spot where I went when I needed to chill out and relax. Friday was my short day of classes along with one of my days off from work.

I needed all the relaxing I could get after what had happened last night with Mom.

She'd shown up at my apartment early yesterday evening with Lila in tow, ready to give me the guilt trip to end all guilt trips. She'd wasted no time in getting to the point of why she'd been there, making comments about Jacob and how she'd done her research and found out who he was, what he did for a living.

My phone buzzed and my stomach tightened at the sound. I took one last look at the beach, letting the sight of the endless ocean calm me, before reaching into my shoe and taking out my phone.

Where are you? Lila wants to see you and I want to talk.

I rolled my eyes. Lila was six months old. She wanted a bottle and a clean diaper. *Talk about what?* I fired back.

Talk about that fiancé of yours. I don't know about him.

I could sense Mom's angle here. No doubt she saw Jacob as an obstruction to getting what she wanted. If she could, she'd try to get him out of the way – whatever it took.

It doesn't matter if you don't know about him. We're getting married and that's that.

Another instant response. *At least come see me so we can talk about him face-to-face.*

Not a chance in hell. *Sorry. I have school stuff tonight and can't meet you. We'll be over for dinner on Sunday again.*

I shoved my phone back into my shoe and closed my eyes. I would not let my selfish mother ruin my one day to relax.

Another chime sounded from my phone – this time, with a text from Jacob. My heart skipped a beat at the sight of his name.

I want to see you.

That was the extent of the message. I held my phone my hands, unsure of what to make of his text.

Another one came, the phone buzzing against my fingers.

Now.

A crafty smile formed on my lips at the idea of seeing Jacob again. I took my phone and quickly typed up a text.

Well, what are you going to do about it?

The response came a few moments later.

Pin me your location.

I did. A few seconds passed, another text arriving.

I'll be there in thirty. Be somewhere visible.

I stuck my phone into the back pocket of my jean shorts, stepped into my sneakers, and hurried across the beach back to the boardwalk.

As promised, 30 minutes later a sleek, black luxury sedan pulled in front of me and came to a stop, the windows tinted as dark as the law allowed.

The back passenger side door opened, revealing nothing but

darkness within. Taking a deep breath of anticipation, I slid into the backseat, the door shutting behind me.

Jacob looked great, as usual. He was dressed in dark blue slacks and a crisp, white button-up shirt, the top two buttons undone, the perfect squares of his pecs drawing my eyes in.

His body language suggested he was open and content, his demeanor sending the message that he didn't have a care in the world. Everything about him was effortless and cool and confident.

For someone who was constantly surrounded by awkward, boorish college guys, Jacob was like something from another planet.

Jacob said nothing at first, peering at me from behind his dark sunglasses, that smirk on his face that seemed to be a fixture of his look.

I could tell, even though he wasn't saying a word, that he was gazing at me with hungry eyes. Knowing he desired me made my pussy clench in excitement and arousal.

We drove, silence lingering in the air.

I cleared my throat and spoke, the quiet becoming too much to take.

"So, there's another dinner coming up this Sunday. That's going to be status quo for the next month or two until this is all over and done. Normally, I'd tell Mom to screw off and leave me alone. But it's the only way I'm going to be able to see Lila and Mom knows it, which is the worst part."

Jacob said nothing, my words still hanging in the air. The car turned another corner.

Just as I was about to ask him what the hell was going on, he smoothly slid across the seat, stopping right next to me. Before I knew it, his hand was on my thigh and his lips on mine.

I melted into the kiss, despite the abruptness of it. I closed my eyes and opened my mouth and let his tongue find mine, his musky flavor washing over me.

Suddenly, I came to my senses in the middle of the kiss, placing my hands on his broad shoulders and pulling away.

"Sunday," I said. "You got that?"

He grinned. "I got it."

I smiled. "Good. And...where are we going?"

"Dinner," he said. "Made reservations. But we're taking the long way."

"Good."

The kiss went on, quickly turning into much more.

CHAPTER 12

JACOB

That Sunday was just as painful as the last. Naomi had wasted no time in grilling me about my personal and work life. It was a surprise to find that she didn't mention to the rest of the family just who I was and how I made my money.

She was holding back, and I could only guess at her motivations for why. I knew there was a good chance she had something planned with the information and was waiting for just the right moment to drop it. For the time being though, she kept it to herself.

Delilah held her own as usual.

Her mother once again went through the routine of trying to get her to part with her money, to make promises about how she'd "lend" some cash to her and Sam when she finally had access to her trust.

Delilah hadn't budged. She'd stuck to her guns and told her mother that no, her mind hadn't changed. I could only imagine how hard that must've been for her, Lila sitting on her lap as she laid down the law to her mother. Though it'd been admirable as hell to see.

So far, the plan was working. My presence gave Delilah the little push that she'd needed to find her backbone. With each day that passed, we were a little bit closer to her birthday. Once that arrived, she'd have access to her money and be able to invest it as she saw fit.

Though it'd been a lie when I'd mentioned it during that first dinner, I decided that it was a good idea to put her in touch with one my accountants. It wouldn't hurt to give her a little expert help when it came to the inheritance of a massive amount of money.

After the dinner with her family, I'd taken her back to her apartment where we'd ended up in bed.

I'd never been with a woman like Delilah before, a woman who was as explosive in bed as she was. It didn't matter that I'd been the first man she'd been with – the chemistry between us was unlike anything I'd ever experienced.

After a few days, I found I was missing her and sent a text.

Any chance I can see you today?

At work right now then study later. Coffee?

I pulled into one of the spots in front of Culprit Coffee, the day warm with a perfect, blue sky above. The coffee shop seemed to be less busy than normal, which was perfect for my intentions. I strolled in and noticed a single employee was behind the counter, a pretty-ish woman in her late twenties who smiled as I entered. The tag on her apron read "Megan."

"Hi!" she said, her smile broad and toothy. "Welcome to Culprit!"

"Hi," I said as I approached the counter. "I have a bit of an odd request."

"We love odd requests. What can I do for you?"

"I was here about a week ago and tasted what had to be the best damn latte of my life."

"Not surprising," she said. "That's what we do. One latte, then?"

"Yes, but here's the odd part. I wanted to know if the woman who made it could, well, make it again for me. I'm sure you do excellent work, but all the same I'd like to see if she'd be able to repeat the magic again."

"Well, what's her name?"

"Delilah."

Megan smiled. "One sec."

A moment after Megan ducked into the back, Delilah appeared like a damn vision. "No apron?" I asked. "Someone's out of uniform."

She glanced down and then laughed. "You going to write me up?"

"Just the kinds of things you notice when you're a business owner," I said with a cocky grin. "Anyway, I'll take a latte."

Delilah grinned back. "Coming right up sir."

Sir.

I needed her like mad.

"Ugh, Sean didn't refill the milk again," she complained. "Just a sec, I have to run in back."

I watched her walk away, enjoying the view, as Megan came back to the front and smiled, stepping up to take a customer's order.

With Megan occupied, I made my move. I stepped away from the counter, heading to the door leading from the front of the house to the back.

I opened and stepped through, quickly walking toward the back.

Delilah turned in time to see me approach, a look of surprise on her face.

"Jacob," she whisper-scolded.

I closed the distance between us, putting my hands on her hips. She pulled a gasp of surprise into her mouth, and I brought my lips to the bare incline of her neck and kissed hard.

Her protests ceased as I ran my hand up under her skirt and slipped it into her panties. "This is a bad idea," she spoke through her moans. "We're going to get caught..."

I said nothing, letting my hand do the talking as I spread her wet lips open and moved inside of her. She gasped, the gasp shifting into a moan as I moved deeper inside, her hips bucking against me as I curled my finger in such an angle that allowed me to press gently on her G-spot.

"Oh God, Jacob, right the—" She didn't even get a chance to

finish the sentence before an orgasm shuddered through her body, her legs shaking and her muscles tensing and releasing. Then she let out a sigh, her head hanging forward, her forehead pressing against my shoulder.

I slipped my fingers out of her, pulling her panties back to where they belonged and letting her skirt fall over her legs.

"Now," I said, after kissing her one last time on the neck. "Are you going to make me that latte or do I need to speak to your manager?"

She smiled over her shoulder. "Asshole," she said with a laugh.

CHAPTER 13

DELILAH

The rest of the week flew by. Unfortunately, the sexy encounter with Jacob at work had been the only highlight. The rest of my time was spent working or studying or trying to somehow study while at work.

Jacob lingered in my mind. I couldn't go into the back at work without getting wet thinking about his hands all over me – and inside of me.

Before I knew it, Sunday had arrived, and another dinner was coming up.

I was just about at the end of my shift, wiping off the espresso machines after a particularly harsh rush. In the middle of my cleaning, I paused. A wave of nausea ran through me as intense as it was sudden.

"You alright?"

I turned to see Sean standing nearby, an expression of concern on his face as he took in the sight of me.

"I think so."

"You looked like you were about to throw up. Your face got tense, like this..." Sean winced, sticking out his tongue and gagging in a way that was far more exaggerated than I'd been. I couldn't help but laugh.

"That's *not* what I looked like – come on."

"OK, not that bad. But you looked a little green for a second."

I shook my head. "It's nothing. Just some nausea out of nowhere."

He didn't seem entirely convinced. "Well, feel free to lie down in the breakroom for a few minutes if you need to. I can come get you if we're busy."

"Thanks, but I'm fine."

He shrugged. "Sure. Offer still stands."

I went back to work, trying to put the strange nausea out of my head.

It returned a couple of times, quick spasms of intense ick that made me feel for a second like I might actually throw up. That never came to pass, thankfully, and I managed to get on with the rest of my shift.

A text from Maryann came around two, a smile forming on my lips when I read what she wrote.

Got some good news – Mom's not feeling well today. Dinner's off.

Relief washed over me. Not having to deal with Mom and Sam grilling me about money, if only for one night, was about the best possible thing I could hear.

Another text quickly followed.

Mom wanted us to take Lila for the night. So, Corrine and I were thinking about grabbing some dinner. You want to come?

A night out with my sisters sounded great. I sent a quick text to Jacob to let him know there'd been a change in plans.

Hey! Dinner's off tonight. Going out to eat with my sisters. As I typed, I realized that I still really wanted to see him. *Want to do something after?*

He didn't make me wait long for his reply.

You know I want to see you. I'll come by at 8.

A grin spread across my face from ear to ear. My night was looking up.

~

A few hours later, Corrine and Maryann and I were seated at an outdoor table at Le Beurre, a little bistro near where Maryann lived in Santa Monica. The patio faced the water, the thin band of ocean in the distance glittering with light from the setting sun. Corrine was next to me, Lila on her lap as Corrine did her best to prevent our little sister from grabbing everything on the table.

The three of us had been chatting about one thing or another, picking at our small salads as we did. It had been infinitely preferable to an evening with Mom. But during the middle of our meal, Maryann set down her fork and sighed, glancing over to Corrine, the two of them sharing a look that made it clear they both had the same thing on their minds.

I had a good idea what it was.

"So," Maryann said. "About Jacob..."

I decided to get right into it. "Look, I know what you both are thinking."

My sisters shared another look.

"What?" I asked.

"Nothing!" Corrine said. "It's just that..." She trailed off.

"There's an age difference." Maryann was never one to beat around the bush. "And it's a pretty big one."

"So?" I asked. "It's not *that* big. He's only..." I let my words hang in the air, realizing that I didn't even know his age. "Um, thirty-five."

"And you're not even twenty-one yet!" Maryann said. "You don't think that's a little extreme?"

"Not really. I mean, age gaps like that were totally common back in the day. Wasn't grandma barely an adult when grandpa married her when he was almost thirty?"

"That was a long time ago," Corrine said. "It's twenty twenty-two – things are different now."

I waved my hand through the air, not wanting to get embroiled in an argument.

"It's fine. He's older than me, sure. But what's so bad about that? Would you rather me date one of those dudes from school who still think that getting wasted on a Tuesday is the coolest thing in the world? Jacob is great – he's mature, he's sophisticated, he's been around. And he's already got his career sorted out. And you can't tell me he's not totally hot."

My sisters shared another look that suggested they knew I had a point.

"I mean, he is," Corrine said. "But...how long have you even known each other? For the last few months, you've been too busy with work and school to hang out with us more than once a month. And now you're engaged. I know the heart wants what it wants and all, but this was fast."

"You're right, it all happened fast. But isn't that the dream? One day you're living your usual, boring life, then out of nowhere you meet the perfect guy, and he sweeps you off your feet. Before you know it, you're in love. Well, that's what happened to me. And I can tell you this – I haven't been this happy in a long, long time."

The more I spoke, the more I realized there was actual truth to what I was saying. Jacob *was* amazing; he *had* swept me off my feet.

Maryann sighed, the tone of her sigh suggesting she'd realized that she was out of line.

"Listen – I'm sorry. I don't mean to give you the third degree about all this stuff, but I wouldn't be doing my job as your older sister if I didn't, you know?"

"We just want what's best for you," Corrine added.

Lila let out a ba-ba-ba of baby babble, as if she were throwing her two cents into the mix.

I smiled. "I know you do. And I love you both like crazy for it."

With that, the conversation dropped, the remainder of the dinner finishing smoothly.

As we wrapped up and went our separate ways, I made a vow to not lie to my sisters for any longer than was absolutely necessary.

Once I had access to my money and could safely store it away, I'd let them in on what was really going on with Jacob and me.

I walked into my apartment and pulled out my phone to text Jacob but saw a message already waiting for me.

Be there in five.

I chuckled at the sight of it.

Five minutes wasn't nearly enough time to change, so I stayed in the pair of cutoff shorts and the T-shirt I had on.

I gave myself a quick once over in the mirror to make sure I looked decent, and by the time that was done I heard the now familiar growl of his sports car outside of my building.

A big smile spread across my face as I grabbed my purse, keys and phone and hurried out of my apartment.

Jacob was out front leaning against his car. He had on a black T-shirt and black leather racing jacket, dark jeans and black boots. The man always managed to look effortlessly cool and sophisticated all the time.

The faintest hint of a grin formed on his lips as I approached, his eyes moving up and down my body.

"Evening," he said as I came closer.

"Evening."

I stepped on my tiptoes and planted a kiss on his lips. He wasted no time putting his hands on my hips and leaning in, opening his mouth, and turning the kiss into something far more than a simple greeting.

My pussy tightened as he kissed me long and deep, soaking through my panties.

He was hard, too. I could feel his stiffness through his jeans against my leg. A moan slipped out of my mouth at the sensation of his cock against me. I didn't know what he had planned for the night, but I was quickly imagining what I wanted to do.

"Get in." He broke the kiss and opened the door for me.

When we were both in the car, he revved the engine and pulled onto the main road. He took a right, and then another right.

I was confused – he'd merely made a big circle around my apartment.

He pulled into the alley between my building and the one next to it. There was no one around, the windows for the first floor high up enough that no one could see us.

"Take off your shorts."

"Huh?"

"Your shorts. I want you out of them."

His gruff voice sent a wave of arousal through my body, and I couldn't help but undo the button of my jean shorts and shimmy them down my legs. The light pink pair of panties I had on underneath on full display, I waited with wide eyes for what he was going to ask me next.

He didn't say a word. Instead, he reached over and placed his hand between my legs, his fingers teasing my clit through my soaked panties.

I moaned, closing my eyes, and letting him touch me the way he wanted, letting him bring me closer and closer to orgasm.

I was so turned on from the kiss that it took no time at all for me to come. I shuddered in my seat, letting out little shrieks that I hoped no one near the alley had heard.

When I was done, my chest rising and falling, I turned toward him.

"Take off your panties."

I happily complied. He pulled the seat back, then opened up his zipper and inched his pants down. His cock, thick and long and glorious as ever, sprang out rock-hard. I bit down on my lower lip at the sight of it, wanting nothing more than for it to be buried inside of me.

"Come here."

He didn't need to tell me twice. I took off my seat belt and sidled my way over. Once I was near, he clamped his hands down on my hips and quickly put me in position over his cock. I reached down and took hold of him, the sensation of his thickness causing another moan to pour from me. He gazed at my body with hungry eyes as he pulled off my shirt.

I lowered myself down, my pussy fully ready to take him inside. I was so impossibly wet by this point that he glided in me with little effort, tingles spreading throughout as he filled me in only the way he could.

When he was fully buried, I leaned my head on his shoulder as he undid my bra and slipped it off.

"I want you to ride me," he said. "Hard."

The way he felt inside was so intense that I couldn't do anything but nod to show I understood. I started by wriggling my hips a bit as he scooped my pert breasts into his hands and rubbed my nipples in a way that made them hard within seconds.

I lifted my ass and brought my body down, the quick driving of his cock straight into me so pleasurable that I knew it wouldn't take long before I came again.

He put his hands on my ass, squeezing me hard as he lifted my body again. I came down on him once more, his cock vanishing inside of me.

I moaned. "God, you feel so good," I said before covering his stubbly cheek in kisses.

His hands moved over the smoothness of my back, as if he wanted to make sure every inch of my body was attended to. I moved faster, my hips bucking as I brought him into me again and again.

The pleasure blasted through me as the orgasm broke, Jacob letting out a hard grunt as he put his hands on my ass once more, bringing me against him as his cock pulsed with his own climax.

I savored the way he felt as he unloaded inside of me, his balls draining deep within.

Our pleasure faded and I leaned forward, his seed trickling out of me as I rested my head on his shoulder.

"I wonder if anyone saw us," I asked, looking around with a grin.

He held me close, which was all I really wanted.

CHAPTER 14

JACOB

The rest of the evening was wonderful. After our fun in the car, I took her to one of my favorite places in the city – a hole-in-the-wall Korean BBQ joint in Silver Lake where I knew most of the staff. Over ribs and bulgogi beef, we caught up on what was going on with our lives.

As we spoke, I realized that I didn't really have anyone like her in my life, someone with whom I could grab a bite and just *be*.

As close as Archie and I were, there was still a professional distance.

I preferred it that way.

That is, until I'd met Delilah.

"I need to tell you something," I said.

She popped a piece of bulgogi into her mouth with her chopsticks and cocked her head to the side.

"What?"

"I'm going to be out of town for the next week."

"You are?"

"That going to be a problem?"

She glanced aside, thinking over the question.

"I mean, no – you've got your business to run. And...I assume this is a business thing, right?"

A tinge of curiosity was in her voice. I wondered if she was thinking that I might be meeting with another woman.

In the past, with anyone else, I wouldn't have cared but I didn't want to play games with Delilah.

"It's a business thing. I'm flying over to Vegas to meet with an associate who wants me to invest in a new club he's opening. He wants to show me the town while I'm there."

She nodded, understanding. "And does that mean you're going to be gone this upcoming Sunday?"

"Yes. I'm leaving tomorrow morning, and I'll be back in exactly a week. Listen, if it's your mother you're worried about, you're more than capable of handling her on your own. You've got your story, and you've got me."

She nodded.

"And...there's something else."

"What is it?"

"It's something that I was planning on giving to you when I got back into town. Call it a...secret weapon."

She leaned forward, an intrigued smile on her face.

"You've got my interest. Tell me more."

"I'd rather show you. Only thing is that it's at my place."

Her eyes flashed with excitement. "Your place? I've never seen your place before. I don't even know what part of town you live in."

"I'm downtown. But I should warn you – it's not really set up for guests."

"What does that mean?" she asked with a smile. "Total bachelor pad? Lots of pizza boxes and empty beer bottles everywhere?"

I couldn't help but let out a laugh at her questions. "Not quite. More like it's not the warmest place in the world. You'll see what I mean when we get there."

"Then let's not waste another second."

The night was pleasant, so I put the convertible top down as I drove toward the lights of the city.

My place was one of the newer buildings in the area, an ultra-modern condo right in the middle of downtown. I pulled my car into my reserved spot near the elevator. We rode that all the way up, the doors opening directly to my place.

"Holy crap," she said as she stepped out of the elevator. "This is unbelievable."

It was a two-story penthouse, the square footage enough to qualify it as a mansion in the sky. The walls were glass, allowing for sweeping views of the city.

The view was especially dramatic at night, the towers of downtown glittering, the sprawl of LA endless around us.

"Thanks," I said. "Something to drink?"

She shrugged. "Whatever is fine."

I made my way into the enormous kitchen. I opened the fridge and saw that, to my dismay, there was nothing inside but bottled water and a six-pack of craft beers that I'd picked up a few months back but never finished.

I grabbed a bottle of water for her and one of the beers for me.

When I returned to the main room, I saw that Delilah had gone out onto the huge balcony.

I took the opportunity to step into my office, opening the safe under my desk and taking out the surprise I had for her. That in hand, I went out to the balcony, the drinks in one hand and the surprise in the other.

She turned as I came out, her perfect body outlined by the city behind her. I handed Delilah the drink and she took it with a smile.

"Thanks. And you know...I don't think the LAPD would exactly be kicking down the doors of this place if you were to offer me a beer."

I chuckled as I took a sip. "What can I say? I run a club and serving minors on accident is one of the easiest ways to get your business screwed up for a month. Old habits die hard, I suppose. Just you wait – I'll have a bottle of Veuve set aside for when you finally turn twenty-one."

She smiled. "I'm going to hold you to that." Delilah pursed her lips. "So, what's this surprise that you brought me over for?"

I took a sip of my beer and set it down on one of the nearby tables. I slipped the small, black box out of my pocket.

Her eyes went to it right away, her gaze going wide.

"Is that what I think it is?"

"Open it and find out."

She took the box from my hands, popping the top. Her eyes turned into saucers as she took in the sight of the massive diamond.

"This is the biggest damn rock I've ever seen in my life."

Glancing up at me one more time, she took the ring out of the box and placed it on her finger. The diamond was huge, almost comically so.

"I figured that we needed a little something to really sell this fake engagement thing," I said.

She smiled, shaking her head. "This has to be two carats, if not more."

"Three, to be exact."

When I said the words, the smile faded from her face.

"Please, please don't tell me you spent God only knows how much on this ring just to make our fake engagement seem more believable."

"Don't worry – I didn't spend a penny."

She cocked her head to the side, confused. "Then...what? Did you have someone lend it to you? If so, this might be a little much to be going around the city with. I don't want to lose it or anything."

"Not quite. One of my former regulars was a prince of one of the Saudi royal families. He came in whenever he was in town, spending money like crazy. In time, I found out why he was so into my humble club – he was in love with one of my dancers.

"Anyway, one night he decided to make his intentions known in the only way he understood how – by flashing his money. He came in with this ring, offered it to my dancer, and proposed on the spot."

"What happened?"

"Well, you're holding the ring – that should be a big clue right there. Turns out she was already married. When he found out and realized that he couldn't just buy her affection, he threw the ring on the ground and stormed out. Never saw the guy again. Archie grabbed it and gave it to me. Been hanging onto it ever since. Figured by this point, the guy doesn't want it back. So, go ahead and wear it while we sell this fake engagement to your mom."

She stuck out her hand and looked at it again.

"It's beautiful. A little gaudy, but pretty all the same."

"Not what you'd pick out."

She let her hand drop. "If it were up to me, I'd have my grandma's old engagement ring. It's this beautiful family heirloom that she's been keeping."

"Then she might not be happy about this giant thing."

"She's in London. Hopefully, this fake story will be over before she finds out about any of this nonsense. And besides, I've got no guarantee she'd even give it to me." She glanced at the ring one more time. "But I don't want to sound spoiled. A massive ring like this will be perfect for our fake romance."

"Good." I wrapped my arm around her hip and planted a kiss on her lips.

As I stood there with her, the two of us gazing out over the city, I found myself wondering just how fake this romance was turning out to be.

CHAPTER 15

DELILAH

The week moved by at an impossible crawl. I knew that I shouldn't have been feeling this sort of way, but I couldn't wait for Jacob to get back.

The idea scared me a little. The whole relationship was supposed to be a farce, but the way I was starting to feel about him was anything but.

It was Sunday, and I was at work in the break room, a barely touched plastic bowl of pad Thai in front of me as I flipped through our text conversation over the last week.

I went through the media tab, shaking my head in disbelief at the shot of me in my bedroom in nothing but a pair of panties, my phone in one hand and my boobs in the other.

I scrolled a little further in the media tab, coming to a stop on the most recent picture he'd sent me. It was a POV shot of him lounging by the private pool of his penthouse hotel room. He wore a pair of black Speedo-style shorts, his cock straining against the spandex, the Vegas strip in the distance. It was more than enough to make me totally wet right there at work.

Another text came in as I was drooling over the first. I eagerly clicked over to see that it was another picture from Jacob. This one was him in front of the floor-length mirror in his bathroom, a smirk on his face and nothing but a pair of blue swim shorts on.

Pool's fun. But you here in a bikini would be a nice improvement.

I grinned, feeling another wave of tingles spread out from between my legs. The smile still on my face, I typed up a response.

Doesn't seem like you're doing much *work* on this little business trip.

The three periods of an incoming text appeared, followed by the response.

Plenty of time for work and play. You could learn a thing or two from me.

That got a laugh out of me.

Hard to play when you're in the middle of a shift at a coffee shop, you know. I followed that with a wink emoji.

Another quick response.

Give it a try. I bet you can pull it off.

I pursed my lips and looked around, as if there might be someone looking over my shoulder.

The coast was clear, and I wasted no time springing out of my seat and hurrying to the small bathroom attached to the break room. Once inside with the door shut, I undid the back of my apron and pulled it up, along with the front of my shirt.

Next, I undid the button of my jeans and opened the zipper a bit, just enough to give a hint of the light pink panties I had on. I pulled the cup of one bra up enough to expose my breast, then took a quick shot of myself in the mirror.

Moments later, I was dressed and back in the breakroom.

I shook my head as I went through the pictures, unable to believe that Jacob had managed to bring out such a side of me. I picked the one I liked the best and sent it.

How's this for work and play?

Exactly what I had in mind.

Is that all you have in mind?

Not quite. Now I'm thinking about all the things I want to do to you.

A thrill ran up my spine.

Like what?

You'll find out when I get back.

It was too much to take. I "hearted" the message and stuck my phone back into my pocket. I was turned on like crazy, no idea how I'd be able to make it through the rest of the shift.

Suddenly, the nausea returned. I shot up from my seat once more, the feeling so intense that I could hardly stand it.

Before I could decide whether or not I wanted to run to the bathroom, the door to the break room opened and Megan stuck her head inside.

"Hey!" she said. "I know you're on your break, but your friend Laura's here. Figured you'd want to know."

My hand on my stomach, I took one deep breath and then another. Just like it had the other times, the nausea passed.

"You alright?" Megan asked.

I nodded quickly. "Yeah, fine. Just got some heartburn or something."

"Oh, you know what's good for that? Baking soda in water. Let me know if you want some."

Megan's helpfulness managed to put a smile on my face. "Thanks. But I think I'm good for now. Can you tell Laura I'll be out in a sec?"

Megan gave me a thumbs-up before leaving me alone. I stepped into the bathroom one more time, washing my face and making sure I looked halfway presentable.

"Hey!" Laura had an eager expression on her face as I stepped out of the back. "What's up?"

A quick glance of the rest of the café let me know that we were still pretty dead.

"You're looking at it," I said. I glanced back at Megan. "Mind if I take the rest of my break outside?"

"Go for it," Megan said. "Take an extra five if you want – not like I need you on the floor."

I grabbed myself a coffee, going outside with Laura and sitting at a table in the empty patio.

Laura leaned in, a scheming expression on her face.

"So...let's hear it."

"Hear what?"

She laughed. "Don't tell me you're going to be coy. You know what, or *who*, I'm talking about."

I glanced away, trying to think of how to even begin discussing the matter. I traced the top of my coffee cup with my fingertip, buying myself a moment to put some words together.

"I don't know. This whole thing started off as a business arrangement, right? I give him some money, he comes to dinner with me a few times and backs me up while I put my mom in her place, and that was the end of it."

"But that *wasn't* the end of it," she said with a grin. "Because now you're totally in love with the guy."

"No way!" The words shot out of my mouth. "Not even close to being in love with him. It's more like...this arrangement went in some directions that I hadn't expected."

"What kind of directions?"

"Like..."

I didn't get a chance to finish. Another wave of nausea hit me, and this time it hit me hard. My eyes flashed wide, and I sprang out of my seat, not wasting a moment before hurrying off the patio and back into the café.

"You alright?" Megan called out after me as I rushed into the bathroom.

I dropped to my knees and let loose, emptying my stomach.

"Hey, you OK?"

Megan and Laura stood behind me, concerned expressions on their faces.

Embarrassed, I grabbed a handful of toilet paper and wiped my mouth with it before pushing myself up off the floor.

I shook my head, not wanting to make a thing out of it. "It's nothing. Something I ate must not have agreed with me. I can get back out there."

Megan was insistent. "Not a chance. Get out of here, go home and get some rest."

"But—"

Megan shook her head, cutting me off. "No discussion. We're having a slow day, and I can handle things for a half an hour until Sean gets here. Now, go on and get out of here."

I gave her a weak smile. "Thanks."

Megan smiled back at me as I passed, asking if I needed anything before I left. I told her no, and that I'd be in touch if things got worse and I needed another day off. But by the time we were in Laura's Miata and on our way, I already felt a ton better.

"Alright," she said. "We're going to get you a pregnancy test."

I couldn't believe what I'd just heard.

"We're...what?"

She flashed me a smirk. "You heard me. We're getting you a pregnancy test. Hell, we're getting you three of them."

"Why do I feel like there was a whole conversation that happened in your own head?"

"Because I know that you were about to tell me that you'd slept with Jacob." She raised a finger toward me as we drove. "And don't even try to tell me that's not what you were going to say."

I bit my lip, knowing she had me.

"But I'm on the pill," I protested.

"And the pill is only ninety-eight percent effective," she countered. "That pesky two percent can be a real bitch."

She pulled to a stop in front of CVS.

"Congrats on finally losing your virginity, by the way."

I let out a grunt of a laugh.

"Thanks."

Twenty minutes later we were back at my apartment, three pregnancy tests in front of us on the coffee table in the living room.

I groaned, tension building in me.

"Alright, let me do it."

I took the three tests out of their packages and headed into the bathroom. The tests were instant – I didn't need to wait more than a minute to get the results.

They were all positive.

What the hell was my fake fiancé going to think about a very real baby?

CHAPTER 16

JACOB

I never took my phone into a meeting.

I got back to my room to discover several missed calls and texts from Delilah that had me worried.

Hey.

You there?

Sorry to bother you, but it's important.

Can you pick up? Please?

Without wasting another second, I called. Her phone rang and rang, and each time it did without her answering, I was tempted to charter a helicopter home.

Finally, there was an answer.

But it wasn't Delilah.

"Hello?"

"Who is this?" I asked. "Where's Delilah?"

"Hey, is this Jacob? This is Delilah's friend, Laura."

"Is everything alright there?"

"Delilah's OK. But she's sleeping at the moment."

The relief that washed over me was indescribable. I closed my eyes and savored it before continuing.

"Well, if she's alright then, don't wake her."

"I won't, but Jacob, you might want to come see her as soon as you can."

I was a little confused by the statement.

"You said she was alright," I reminded her.

"She is, but I think she needs to see you sooner rather than later."

I could sense there was more she wasn't saying, and I needed to find out what it was.

"If that's the case, give me three hours," I replied.

I hung up and called the number for the helicopter service I used to make trips between LA and Vegas.

After that, I called my associate and told him the meeting for tomorrow was off, that I'd be flying him in so we could meet the following week instead.

Delilah was all that mattered.

I packed my things and met the helicopter on the roof of the hotel. We took off with no trouble, and by the time we were in the air the sun was already going down, the entire western horizon brilliant with wild, orange light.

The flight was about an hour, give or take, and while I'd been in the air, I'd arranged for my car to be waiting for me at the helipad. The sun had set by the time I got behind the wheel, and I wasted no time hauling ass to Delilah's apartment.

I parked and rushed to the front door, knocking softly in the event that Delilah was still resting.

The door opened and Laura placed her finger on her lips in a "shh" gesture. I nodded and entered as she moved out of the way to let me in.

My stomach clenched as I saw Delilah curled up on the couch. Though Laura had reassured me Delilah was alright, I couldn't shake the feeling that something big had happened.

"I'll get going now that you're here," Laura said. "Tell Delilah to call me if she needs anything." With those cryptic words, Laura left.

The apartment was totally silent, quiet enough that I could hear the soft sounds of passing traffic. I stared at Delilah, feelings swirling inside of me that I didn't know what to do with.

Soon, Delilah began stirring, moving on the couch, and opening her eyes slowly. When she saw that I was there, her sleepiness vanished in a moment, her blue eyes flashing with surprise.

"Jacob!" She got up and hurried over to me as I stood up. I wrapped my arms around her and held on tight.

"Delilah," I said. "Whatever it is, tell me. I need to know."

She nodded, blinking her eyes. Tears trickled down her cheeks, and the moments of silence that passed were like torture.

"I'm pregnant."

CHAPTER 17

DELILAH

I hadn't quite known what to expect from Jacob when I'd told him I was pregnant.

He'd been cool about it.

I'd said the words and he'd simply nodded, taking in the information, and thinking it over, not in a stressed-out sort of way, but more like he was filing it internally.

Then he'd said the only words I'd wanted to hear.

"It's going to be fine. I'll take care of everything."

The first decision we made was that I'd be living with him for a time. I knew I could take care of myself but staying with him meant that he'd be there for me if I needed anything, and that I'd be able to rest and relax in a place that was bigger than four-hundred square feet.

I'd told him that I was still going to work, and that was fine with him.

I'd known something was up when he'd asked me the name of my property company, going outside for a moment after I'd told him.

He returned as I was in the process of packing some things to take with me.

"Jacob?" I asked, setting down the sundress I'd just folded. "What did you do?"

"Paid off the rest of your lease," he said.

My eyes went wide. "You *what?*"

"Just what I said. The place is still yours, of course. But the remainder of your year is paid off. Last thing you need to worry about is rent. And I'll do the same with your utilities and such."

I didn't know what to say. "You don't have to do any of that," I said. "I can handle rent and work and bills. Remember I'm about to come into a lot of money and—"

I didn't get a chance to finish before he came over to me and placed his hands on my shoulders.

"Delilah, I know you're independent – and I love that about you. There's no need for you to worry about me keeping you like a bird in a cage in downtown LA."

"But..."

"*But* you're pregnant with my child, and we're in this together. That means you're going to have to get used to me taking care of you. Understand?"

There was a softness to his tone, a warmth that I'd never noticed before. It made me feel like everything truly was going to be OK.

"Now," he said. "Finish packing. Whatever you don't want to bring now, I'll have someone pick up tomorrow. If you want, we can have everything in this place packed up and moved before the end of the day."

"I don't need anything so drastic. But thanks."

He leaned in and kissed me softly, a kiss that made my worries melt away.

"Finish up. We're going to leave as soon as you're ready."

With that, I hurried back into my bedroom and finished throwing the essentials in my biggest suitcase. My mind raced as I packed, all sorts of things occurring to me that I hadn't thought of.

There was the matter of work, not to mention school. How the hell was I supposed to handle my course load while pregnant and then caring for a newborn?

I thought about my family, anxiety running through me at the idea of telling my mom what was going on.

Knowing her, all she'd care about is how it affected the possibility of getting her hands on my money.

I did my best to put all of that out of my mind. There was so much to think about now, and it didn't make a bit of sense to wrap myself up with maybes.

All the same, I wanted to talk to someone. As I packed, I took my phone out of my pocket and sent a quick text to Laura, letting her know what was going on.

Her response came quickly, and it was one full of support. She told me she was there for me no matter what, and if I needed her, not to hesitate.

Warmth filled me as I read the words and I replied with a heart emoji. I still had to tell my sisters, but that could wait for now.

When I was ready, I brought my bag out to the living room where Jacob awaited me, his phone in his hand and an expression of intense concentration on his face. I could tell he was in the zone, whatever he was doing.

"Hey."

He flicked his eyes up to me.

"Just getting things sorted out. Three pregnancy tests are likely as accurate as we need, but I made an appointment with a doctor all the same. It's tomorrow afternoon. I can go with you if you'd like, or I can have a car take you if you'd like a little more privacy."

He glanced aside once he was done speaking, as if a thought had occurred to him.

"But you'll have time to think all that over. For now, let's get you to my house."

I was confused. "Your house? You mean your apartment?"

He shook his head. "No, I mean my house. The apartment downtown isn't my only home – I have a place in Malibu."

My eyes flashed at the news. "Malibu?"

He nodded. "That's right. It's on the beach, not to mention nice and private. It's a bit out of the way, but you'll have access to my driver for whenever you need to come to the city."

"You're not going to get any argument from me about staying in Malibu. I just didn't know you had an extra house laying around." I followed this up with a smile.

He matched my grin with one of his own. "It was my first place before I got the apartment to be closer to work. I told myself I'd go there whenever I needed to decompress, but that doesn't happen all too often."

Jacob flipped his wrist and checked the time on his very nice, very expensive, silver watch. "Anyway, we should get going. We'll order dinner in tonight, and then you can get settled."

"That sounds nice." Part of me had been concerned about being a burden, but the way he was taking care of everything, not showing the slightest trace of frustration, went a long way.

I took one more pass through the apartment to make sure I hadn't forgotten anything important. I reached for my bag to carry it out, but Jacob beat me to it, moving in with surprising speed and grabbing the handle.

"Thanks," I said. "But I can carry my own bag."

"I'm sure you can. But you're pregnant, remember?"

"Yes, I'm pregnant, not disabled."

He offered a small smile. "I know this isn't going to come easy to you, but for the time being you'll need to get used to letting people take care of you."

I chuckled. "Yeah, I guess you're right. But I'm not about to sit around and be doted on all day."

Jacob shook his head. "Never in a million years would I think you'd want that. Now, let's get moving."

He picked up the suitcase, then opened the door for me to step out. The evening air was brisk and still, and a strange fatigue came over me as we walked to Jacob's car.

The stars were clear and brilliant over the water as we drove, but I had a hard time keeping my eyes open.

Maybe it was the pregnancy, maybe it was the events of the day catching up with me, but all I wanted was to lie down and take a long nap.

"School," I said, my voice barely louder than a mumble. "I need... to go to school."

"You're taking tomorrow off," he said. "We've got the doctor's appointment and you're going to need to rest – at least for one day."

I knew he was right. I made the decision in that moment to try to let go a bit, to do what he was asking, to let him help me.

My eyes closed as I watched the Pacific Ocean pass, the water a dark purple that glimmered with moonlight.

"Hey. We're here."

"Huh?"

I opened my eyes slowly. At first, I thought I was looking at something out of a dream.

We were parked in the middle of a big, circular driveway in front of a three-story, ultra-modern home, the building more glass than anything else. A fountain was a few feet away, the water trickling down into the basin. Off in the distance, I could see a winding path that led down to the beach.

"This is your place?"

"Yep. Assuming no squatters broke in while I was gone."

I chuckled a bit as I sat up and stretched.

"Come on – I ordered some food while you were asleep. Should be here in a little bit."

I stepped out of the car, the moon big and round and bright above and casting the place in surreal lighting. Jacob hauled my big bag out and carried it toward the back entrance of the house. As we made our way, I spotted a huge infinity pool.

We stepped into the house, the lights turning on and illuminating the spotless interior. As impressive as his apartment was, the house was something on a whole other level – bigger, more spacious, with a feeling of total seclusion.

"You sure you don't want to check for squatters?" I asked with a wry smile.

"I have a cleaning crew come once a week to take care of the place. If people were living in here, I'd know about it."

The house was decked out with sleek, modern furniture, clean, cool colors dominating. From the back entrance I could see all the way to the giant kitchen, a huge dining table on a raised area in front of it that seemed like it'd easily seat a couple dozen people.

"I usually take meals on the patio," he said, seeing that I was eyeing the huge table. "Don't worry about anything too formal. Anyway, let me show you your room."

Still carrying my bag, toting the enormous piece of luggage as if it weighed nothing at all, he led me to the stairs. We went up to the second floor, then down the hall to a large bedroom.

The room was perfect – and about as big as my entire apartment. The glass wall looked out onto a small balcony and the ocean beyond, the moon a big, silver coin in the sky above. There was a huge bed, a sitting area with a TV, and even a small nook where I could study. And of course, there was an en suite bathroom, almost as large as the bedroom.

"This work?" he asked.

"This is amazing."

"No one will be able to see you through the window, but there's a button here that'll darken the glass if you want to be on the safe side." He reached over and pressed a button next to the door.

"You can still see out, but it's pitch black on the other side." He stepped over and set my bag down next to the bed. "I'm sure you're going to need more things to settle in, but we can work on a list tomorrow. I'll have one of my people swing by the store and pick up whatever you need."

His phone buzzed, and he took it out to check the screen.

"Food's here. Take a moment to check the place out – I'll go down and get everything set up."

"Sure. And...thanks."

"Least I can do."

With that he left. I sat down on the edge of the bed, trying to wrap my head around everything that was happening. It occurred to me how strange it was that he'd given me my own room.

He was the father of my child – wouldn't it make more sense for us to sleep in the same space?

However, the more I thought about it, the more I appreciated the gesture.

Jacob must've known that I'd want a room of my own, no matter what ended up happening between us. It was so much to process, and I did my best to follow his advice of not thinking about it too much.

All the same, I couldn't help but wonder what the next nine months would hold.

CHAPTER 18

JACOB

I'd had no idea what to feed a pregnant woman – it was a situation I'd never had to deal with before in my life. So, I'd ordered a bit of everything, from Mexican to Italian to sandwiches, along with a few other items.

My staff member had brought all of it in and I'd arranged the food on the table. Once everything was out, I realized how silly it was that I'd gotten so much food.

"This is quite a spread."

I glanced up to see that Delilah had emerged from her room. She'd changed, now dressed in an oversized T-shirt and a pair of sleeping shorts that were so short it looked like she wasn't wearing anything.

"I hope you don't mind," she said, noticing that I'd taken note of her clothes. "Felt like being comfy."

"Not a problem at all," I said. "I want you to feel at home. Please, sit."

Her eyes swept over the food one more time as she picked up a plate and reached for a platter of tacos.

"How are you feeling?" I asked, taking a seat near her.

"Part of me wants to eat everything on this table, another part of me wants to crawl under the covers and sleep for a month."

"That's understandable. I would assume that's all normal. I'm sure the doctor will let you know tomorrow if it isn't."

She nodded as she cracked open the bottle of Fiji water I'd placed near her plate.

"How are *you* feeling?" she asked, taking a sip of water.

I opened my mouth, not sure how to answer. I was used to being in control in my life and my business, but this situation was about as far out of my control as it could get.

"I'm...feeling fine. Just concerned about making sure you're taken care of and have everything you need."

She smiled, shaking her head. "I had a feeling you'd dodge the question like that."

"There was no dodging. You asked the question and I told you that I was concerned."

"Right, but that was more you telling me what you planned on *doing*. What I want to know is how you're *feeling*."

"I'm feeling alright. But my focus is more on you and making sure that you are feeling good, feeling what you're supposed to while pregnant."

She took a bit of her taco as I spoke, chewing slowly then swallowing. I reached for a piece of fried chicken.

"OK, I get that," she said. And I certainly appreciate it. Lord knows there're going to be enough people in my life, like my mom, who are more than likely going to make this all about themselves.

"*But...*"

"But all the same, it's important to me to know how you're feeling. Are you excited to be a dad? Scared? Nervous? What's going through your head, and your heart, right now?"

Her question was reasonable, but the truth was I had no idea how to answer. I took a bite of the fried chicken, giving myself a few moments to think. I washed it down with a swig of beer.

"Honestly, I'm feeling a lot of things right now. I'm trying to wrap my mind around the fact that I'm about to be a father, that what began as a "fake" relationship became really real in what seemed like the blink of an eye."

She chuckled. "OK, fair enough. Just promise me that you will keep me in the loop of how you're feeling throughout all of it. We're in this together, you know? And as much as you want to make sure the focus is on me; remember that it took both of us to get here."

"I'll try," I said. "I mean it. Not saying I'm going to be blubbering my emotions all the time, but I'll try to stay open with you on how I'm feeling, good or bad."

"Good. And thank you."

I nodded, going back to my meal.

"Can I ask you something?"

I flicked my eyes up at her as I chewed, nodding a silent "yes" as a response.

"What about your parents?"

I took in a slow breath through my nose as I chewed. She'd touched on a subject that I didn't want to talk about.

I wasn't going to snap at her in the moment, which is what I would've done to anyone else who'd have asked such a personal question.

"They're gone. And that's all you need to know." I was being brusque, but I needed her to understand the topic was off limits.

Her eyes flashed at my response. "Oh. I mean, sorry. You don't have to tell me anything you don't want to. I was just making conversation. You know, trying to get to know the family of my baby's dad."

I said nothing as I went back to my meal. After several long, tense moments, I knew I needed to put her at ease.

"There anything else I can get you?"

She shook her head. "This is fine for now. But thanks."

"I'm going to put together a grocery list, so think about what you might need or want. And your bathroom has a nice, big tub if you want to take a soak."

"Thanks. That sounds great."

We ate in silence, which was fine by me. I had plenty of things to think about, and I could sense she felt the same way.

When we were done, I told her to go relax while I cleaned up. She tried to insist on helping, but I wouldn't hear of it.

"Come on," she said. "Your hearts in the right place, but I don't want to sit around while you do everything for me."

"On any other night, that'd be fine. But I can tell by one look that you're on the verge of passing out."

Delilah looked so tired that I could sense it was a struggle just to keep her eyes open.

"OK, fine – you're right. But I do plan on doing my share around here."

"I'll take you up on that. Now, get some rest. We've got the appointment tomorrow and I'm sure you've got plenty of business to get in order."

"Yeah. Thanks again, Jacob. It really means a lot, how much you're helping me. I'm already wondering how the hell I'd do this on my own."

"You'd manage. No – you'd thrive."

She laughed a bit. "Thanks. Nice of you to say."

I shook my head. "Not just saying it. I make my living sizing people up, being able to figure out what sort of person they are with just a look. And my first impression of you hasn't changed one bit."

"Is that right?"

"Yep. I knew from the moment you stepped into my club that you were the sort of woman who wasn't afraid of anything, the sort of woman who'd been through hard times but had persevered through it all. And nothing you've said or done since then has changed my mind in the slightest."

I wasn't bullshitting her – I meant every last word.

"Thanks. I mean it. With you at my side, I'm feeling even better about getting through this."

"Good. And *I'd* feel even better if you went upstairs to relax and get some sleep. We'll tackle everything else head-on tomorrow morning."

She gave a quick nod. "Got it. Goodnight Jacob."

Before she left, a strange tension hung in the air, one that could only have been broken by a kiss, but I didn't make the move.

If I kissed her there was no chance I would've been able to stop with just that. I'd want more. When it came to Delilah, I couldn't control myself.

"Goodnight, Delilah. Sleep well."

She left with that.

I closed my eyes and savored the lingering scent of her in the air, the same sweet scent that she'd left in my office that first night we'd met, the same scent that drove me wild.

I stepped out of the kitchen and began cleaning up the food on the table. Neither of us had eaten much of anything. I made a mental note to make sure that Delilah had a good diet and didn't skip any meals.

Once everything was packed away in the fridge, I poured myself a glass of whiskey and stepped out onto the back patio. The view from my place was stunning, the sight of the beach and the moon over the water instilling a calm in me that I hadn't felt in a long while.

There was still the matter of work. I had a damn good team of people working for me. Archie could handle the day-to-day operations of Cherry Lane, though I'd need to make sure he was compensated properly.

I'd also been planning on opening a second location in Vegas. Letting him handle matters here would be the perfect tryout to see if he was ready for his own club.

A cough sounded from somewhere above. Soon, the sound turned from a cough to retching.

I set down my drink and hurried back into the house, running up the stairs and making my way to her bedroom. The door was open, but a quick glance inside revealed that she wasn't there – but the en suite bathroom light was on.

"Delilah?" I asked as I entered the bedroom. "You OK?"

More coughing. "In...in here."

I entered the bathroom to see Delilah on her knees in front of the toilet.

"It's fine." She said, sitting up and flushing the toilet. "Just got sick."

I filled a glass of water, handing it over to her as she did her best to get on her feet again.

"The doctor will know what to do for the nausea."

Delilah nodded without saying a word, sipping her water and standing next to me. She put her head on my shoulder and I wrapped my arm around her.

It was all so strange and new, but in a wonderful sort of way I'd never expected.

CHAPTER 19

DELILAH

I awoke that next morning feeling like I was in some kind of dream. At first, my eyes needed time to adjust to the light that poured into the room.

I sat up slowly in the impossibly comfy bed and took a moment to remember just where I was.

The view before me was even more incredible than it had been the night before. The sky was a perfect, clear blue, the water gently lapping onto the shore.

My eyes fixed onto the beach. I opened the door to the balcony and stepped out.

As I looked out onto the shore, I glanced down to see that, without thinking, I'd placed my hand on my belly.

Pregnant.

The word echoed in my mind, excitement and nervousness running through me in equal measure. The events of the previous day came washing over me, and for a moment I felt like I might be overwhelmed by them.

I didn't have that luxury, however. I was going to be a mom.

While I hadn't had the best role model in that department, I knew that there was no time to be fearful.

I would give my child everything my mother hadn't been capable of giving my sisters or me.

I stepped over to the mirror and took in my reflection, giving a firm, confident nod to my image.

We're going to do this, I said aloud. *We're going to be ok.*

Jacob was going to be a part of it all, too. I checked my phone to see what time it was. It was after eight and I wanted to get downstairs and see what he might be up to.

I took a shower first, giving myself a few extra moments of relaxation in the luxury shower, the water pressure from the ultra-high-tech nozzle working out all the kinks in my back.

Afterward, I threw on a light dress of a white and light blue floral pattern, the hem hitting just above my knee, and stepped into a pair of white Chuck Taylors before heading downstairs.

The smell of cooking breakfast hit me right away, sausage and eggs and several other delicious smelling things. I let the scents carry me toward the kitchen, where I spotted Jacob at the stove.

He looked good as ever, dressed in a black button-up shirt and dark blue jeans, the sleeves of his shirt rolled up enough to show off his gorgeous, toned forearms.

Music played on the stereo in the kitchen – I recognized it right away as the Allman Brothers. To my total shock, Jacob was in the middle of humming along to the words.

"Morning."

He glanced back over his shoulder. If he was surprised, he sure didn't show it. Sometimes I wondered if it was possible at all to spook Jacob Nichols.

"Morning." He turned around, giving me a full view of those gorgeous forearms. "Breakfast will be ready in a few. And if you're in the mood for coffee, I can whip you up something." He nodded toward a very fancy-looking espresso machine.

Jacob had wasted no time going to work making sure I had everything I needed to start my day.

"Coffee sounds amazing," I said. "Do you have decaf?"

"I do. And there are plenty of flavors to choose from."

"In that case, I'd love some."

Jacob turned back to the stove, taking the pan off the burner, and placing the eggs onto a plate, along with the sausage. When he placed it in front of me, I noticed that the eggs were unlike any I'd ever seen before – a smooth tube that was a perfect, golden color.

"Is this an omelet?"

"It is – French style. I spent a year in Paris when I was coming up in the business. I'm not the best cook in the world, but I can do a few things right."

He dusted the omelet with a shower of bright green chives. It looked and smelled amazing.

"Thank you," I said. "But what about you?"

He stepped over to the coffee maker and went to work.

"Not much of a breakfast guy. I'm usually good with a cup of coffee or two until lunch. Go ahead and eat – I'll get this started."

Jacob stepped over to the espresso machine, and I turned my attention to the food in front of me. I started with the omelet, the side of my fork cutting through the eggs as if they were made of soft butter. I took a bite, my eyes going wide at the creamy, delicious texture of the food.

"This is amazing!" I said, not even caring that my mouth was full.

He chuckled. "Glad you like it."

After I took another few eager bites of the omelet, I did the same with the sausage. The espresso machine grumbled to life, and after a few minutes, Jacob placed a cup of wonderful-smelling coffee in front of me before making some for himself.

Jacob placed his hands on the other side of the kitchen island where I was seated and glanced away, as if something was on his mind.

"What's up?" I asked.

"Two things. First is that I spoke to the doctor's office. They bumped the appointment up to eleven if that works for you. I figured the sooner the better."

"That works for me."

"Great. The other thing is…I didn't ask you what your plans are with the baby, if you want to keep it or put it up for adoption or what."

There was no doubt in my mind. "I want to keep it."

He raised his eyebrows. "Yeah?"

"Yeah. It's crazy. If you would've asked me a month or so ago if I thought I had room for a kid in my life, I would've said no way. But now that it's actually happening, there's no doubt in my mind what I want to do. I want to keep it; I want to be a mom."

Jacob's expression was strange. He had a look of total relief at my words but appeared to be trying to keep his reaction in check.

"Good. That's good. I…know what it's like to be bounced around from place to place as a kid, not ever knowing for sure if you're wanted. The idea of that same thing happening to a child of mine…" He trailed off and shook his head, as if the idea were too much to even consider. "I'm glad to know you want to keep it."

I was curious as to what his comments meant. Was he talking about himself? The way he'd answered me about his parents drifted back into my thoughts and I knew not to push.

"Anyway, that's all I needed to know," he said. "If you're ready to see this through, then so am I."

He reached across the island and took my hand, squeezing it tight for one long, wonderful moment.

"The day's yours until we head to the doctor – I'd like to be out the door by ten. Feel free to explore the house and do whatever you'd like. My home is your home."

"Thanks. For everything."

He nodded before leaving. I watched as he scooped his laptop off the counter, then headed outside with that and his mug of coffee.

The situation still felt so strange, and I continued to try and wrap my head around it. All the same, the way that Jacob was going out of his way to make sure I felt taken care of had gone a long way toward helping me ease into it.

I finished my breakfast, enjoying the delicious, home-cooked food. Once that was done, I took advantage of the fact that he'd left without cleaning up.

Once the kitchen was spotless, I hopped on my laptop and checked the notes for the classes I was going to miss that day. I hated cutting and made it a rule to never do it unless I had to. I figured that finding out I was going have a freaking baby was as good a reason as they came to take the day off.

It didn't take long for ten o'clock to roll around. Jacob came back inside and together we stepped out into the warm, late morning air.

My eyes went right to the pool, then the beach, a smile forming on my lips when I realized that both were there for me to enjoy whenever I wanted.

As we drove, the nausea that I'd been dealing with returned with a vengeance.

"Pull over," I said as we drove down the PCH back into LA.

"You alright?" he asked.

I took a deep breath. "Just need to throw up."

He wasted no time finding a good spot to pull over, bringing the car to a halt and letting me out. I opened the door and before I could even put a foot on the ground, I let loose with everything that I'd eaten for breakfast. Jacob kept his hand on my back as I emptied my stomach.

I wiped my eyes and then my mouth with a paper towel that Jacob had handed me. Cars whooshed past, the scent of exhaust blending with the fresh scent of sea air.

Finally, I sat up and shut the door.

"Stupid question," he said. "But how're you feeling?"

"I'm fine. Just...try not to smell my breath."

A small smile formed on his lips. "Seriously, I don't know much about pregnancy, so I've got no idea what's normal and what isn't. I'm sure you're fine, but it's important that we're telling the doctor everything."

"I think I'm fine. I just can't keep anything down."

He nodded in understanding. "Let's get there and see what she has to say. Dr. Cunningham is one of the best in the city, so I've got no doubt she'll know what to do."

Truth be told, I was a little worried. I'd known morning sickness was a part of pregnancy, but I thought it was nothing more than a little here and there. The way I'd felt since arriving at Jacob's place... it was the worst nausea I'd ever experienced in my life.

Jacob's presence and calm demeanor put me at ease, as always.

We soon arrived at a sleek, ten-story office building in Culver City. Jacob helped me out of the car, and after a quick trip up the elevator, we were in the offices of Dr. Marjorie Cunningham.

Jacob thanked the receptionist for getting us in on such short notice, and once we'd finished filling out the paperwork we were quickly taken to a room.

Dr. Cunningham was a small, wiry, red-haired woman with sharp, green eyes that glimmered with intelligence and warmth. She stayed in the room as the nurse gave me the expected list of questions, along with taking some blood work, and when that was done Jacob wasted no time asking what had been on both of our minds.

"She's been sick," Jacob said. "Very nauseous."

"I can't keep anything down," I added. "Is it a bad sign?"

As if sensing my anxiety, Dr. Cunningham put up her hand, a small smile forming on her face for the first time since she'd arrived.

"We'll need to keep an eye on your nausea to be certain. But right now, I can tell you with ninety percent certainty that it's standard morning sickness."

"Standard?" Jacob asked.

She nodded. "Morning sickness, like many other pregnancy symptoms, works on a spectrum. Some women get hit hard by it; some get very little at all. From what you've told me so far, you sound like you're part of the former group. Don't worry – morning sickness tends to be a first-trimester sort of thing. In the meantime, take it easy, and make sure you're getting nutrients into your body – as the old cliché goes, you're eating for two, now. I recommend bone broths and soups when your stomach's feeling weak."

Like Jacob's calm demeanor, Dr. Cunningham's easy way of laying it all out for me helped put my mind to rest.

"Thank you, Doctor."

"Of course. If you start experiencing pain or bleeding, that's something I'll need to know about right away. But so far, it sounds like all your symptoms are completely normal."

I felt a million times better. We went through the rest of the appointment, Dr. Cunningham informing Jacob and me about what to expect over the course of the first trimester and beyond and confirming our due date just before Thanksgiving.

When we were done, my next appointment scheduled, I felt a heck of a lot better, both physically and mentally. On the way back, however, we made a stop at a place I hadn't been expecting – a BMW dealership.

"What're we doing here?"

"I'm guessing you're not going to want to be stuck at my house during the entire pregnancy. Not to mention it's nuts that you live in LA and don't have a car."

"Wait, don't tell me you're saying what I think you're saying."

"Let's get out there and kick some tires, see if you can find a color you like. I'm thinking one of the crossovers would be nice, something big to keep you safe and high up."

I shook my head. "No way. I mean, thanks, I appreciate the idea. But I'm not going to let you just buy me a car."

He shrugged, as if it were no big deal at all.

"If you want, you can pay me back when you get your inheritance. But I'd rather handle it all right now. I'll feel better knowing you and the baby are in a safe vehicle."

I scanned the rows of gorgeous cars in every color I could imagine. A trim man in a sharp suit and a big smile on his face was already approaching.

I needed a car like nothing else, especially if I was going to be living in Malibu and going to school.

"Come on," he said. "It'll be fun."

I had to admit, his positive attitude was infectious.

"Alright. But keep the receipt so I know how much I owe you."

CHAPTER 20

JACOB

"Thank you, Jacob. I really do love it."

To my pleasure, I managed to push past her apprehensions and talk Delilah into picking out a car. She settled on a gorgeous ride, a BMW X7, the color midnight blue.

After we signed everything on the dotted line, she hopped in her new car and I hopped into mine, the two of us stopping off at Whole Foods to stock up on all the groceries we'd need for the next few weeks.

Dr. Cunningham had provided us with a list of all sorts of foods to eat and foods to avoid, so we shopped according to that.

Back at home, I put together a simple lunch of sandwiches and sliced fruit. Since Delilah had thrown up her breakfast, she tore into the food with total gusto.

A while later, Delilah and I were in the middle of enjoying some decaf tea on the patio when her eyes had gone wide with shock, and she ran back into the house and into the nearest bathroom.

Afterward, I heated up some bone broth for her to sip on. That managed to stay down.

"Thank you," she said after she finished the broth. "I hate that you have to see me like this."

"I'm sorry you're going through it."

I hated seeing Delilah suffer like that, knowing I couldn't really help her. I was used to taking charge and doing whatever it took to get things done.

With this pregnancy, that wasn't an option. I could make sure she had food and whatever other comforts she needed, but that was the extent of it for my involvement in the physical process.

After taking a bath to relax, Delilah spent the afternoon on the couch in her pajamas, sipping her bone broth and watching TV. Each sip she managed to keep down was a little more nutrition for our child.

I'd never been the nurturing type, but Delilah made me want to take care of her. To be close to her. She was affecting me in ways I'd never known before.

My life to this point had been about me. I'd worked my way up from the bottom of the club industry in LA, clawing and pushing until I was the owner of one of the most successful gentlemen's clubs in the western hemisphere.

With Delilah, all of that had changed. For once, someone else's concerns and needs took priority over my own.

It was thrilling in a way I'd never experienced before in my life.

"Figures," she said as we were enjoying the evening sun on the patio.

"What's that?"

She smirked. "That I'd get pregnant the first time I had sex."

"They say it only takes one time," I quipped.

"Maybe that means it was meant to be?" she asked. "Or maybe I'm just being silly."

I reached over and took her hand. "If it's happening, then it was meant to be."

"I honestly can't wait to meet our little Thanksgiving turkey."

I couldn't help but smile.

We passed the time watching the water come in, and when a touch of chill appeared in the air, we headed back inside to watch a little TV on the big sectional couch.

The simple act of watching TV with Delilah relaxed me in a way I hadn't been in a long time.

"So," she said once her program ended. "There's something else that we need to talk about."

"What's that?"

She took a deep breath, as if she didn't want to share what was on her mind.

"There's the little matter of my mom. I need to tell her that I'm pregnant."

She was right.

"Yes, but you don't have to tell her until you're absolutely ready."

She shook her head. "I want to tell my family as soon as possible; I want my sisters to know. Besides, maybe this will actually get my mom to back off about the money now that I've got a kid of my own to take care of."

I reached over and took her hand. "You know that you're not going to have to worry about anything, right? Whatever you need, I'll handle it."

She pursed her lips and looked down. "That's...I know. And I appreciate it like crazy. But I'll have more than enough of my own money, plus my education, and eventually a career. I won't rely on anyone else to provide for me."

I nodded. "Then you can have that. And I'll help you in whatever way I can through it all. If you need to take some time off school, you can do that and get right back into it when you're ready."

She brought her blue eyes up to mine, squeezing my hand. "Thank you. I mean it."

"And if you want to tell your family this Sunday, then we can do that. And I'll be right there by your side when it happens."

Delilah leaned over and kissed me, the first kiss we'd shared since she'd arrived. My mouth opened and so did hers, and I found myself wrapping my arm around her waist and guiding her onto her back.

My cock stiffened in seconds, and all I could think about was getting her naked as quickly as possible.

Before we could move too far along, my phone buzzed in my pocket.

"Damnit," I said, reaching for my phone and reading the text from Archie.

Still on for the meeting?

It was ten after three, which meant that I was late – I was never late.

I looked down at Delilah, her honey-brown hair spread out all around her impossibly gorgeous face, an expression of concern on her features.

"Everything OK?"

"Yeah. Just need to take a raincheck on this." I held up my phone. "Meeting to talk about how things are going to be handled at the club now that I'm going to be working from home a little more often."

"Got it. And yeah, let's definitely revisit this subject when you get back." She slipped her hands into my thick hair and brought me down for another deep kiss.

I savored the kiss, drinking her in as if it were the last time I would see her. With a little bit of willpower, I pulled myself away and headed upstairs to my office.

I called Archie on FaceTime and put the image on the big screen.

"There's the man," he said. "And check out those digs – very nice."

I glanced behind me, noticing that the view from his end looked out onto the balcony and the beach beyond.

"Hey, you play your cards right and you'll have a view like this before the year's out."

"Alright, alright," Archie said. "You've got my attention. So, what's the plan?"

"Plan is this – you're handling day-to-day operations at Cherry

Lane for the time being. I'll be available to help, and I will also be stopping in when I can to make sure the place is in order. But for the most part, this is your show, Arch."

"OK," he said, nodding slowly, taking in the massive news I'd just dumped on him. "For how long?"

"The next eight months at least."

"Eight months?" he asked with shock. I winced as I realized I'd inadvertently given away the news.

I chuckled to myself. Normally, I was a damn expert at playing things close to the chest, but with Delilah, all of that was out the window.

"Yeah. Delilah's pregnant."

Archie's eyes flashed with excitement. "You serious, boss? Congrats! This is freaking huge!"

"I know, I know. And thanks." I raised my finger. "You're one of the few people to know, so keep this under your hat."

"Got it. But man, the staff's going to go crazy when they find out the boss is going to be a dad. Might be more than a few disappointed girls, though."

"We'll handle that when the time comes. Right now, I'm focusing on Delilah and making sure she's got everything she needs. I'll be here in Malibu for the time being, so we'll be doing a meeting like this every morning just to make sure everything's running smoothly. And if the next year or so goes well, you can plan on a transfer to Vegas to run the newest branch of Cherry Lane."

Archie nodded, clearly having a hard time hiding the smile on his face.

"I like where this is heading. But let me ask you this – how the hell am I going to get a view like that living in the middle of the desert?" He grinned after he spoke, letting me know he was only joking.

"Hey, you run Cherry Lane in Vegas as well as you can and be smart with the money you earn, you'll be able to buy the house next to mine before you know it."

"I like it."

We wrapped up the call, and I grabbed a bottle of water from the office fridge then stepped out onto the balcony. I sipped my drink and looked out at the ocean, still wrapping my mind around how my life had changed so abruptly.

I smiled as I remembered the beautiful woman downstairs waiting to finish what we'd started.

CHAPTER 21

DELILAH

The next few days passed in a blur. Thankfully, the worst of the nausea subsided and by Wednesday I was able to get back to class and work.

I'd spoken to Megan, letting her know that I was pregnant and that I would need a reduction in my hours.

Thankfully, she was totally cool with it. She told me she'd take me down to two shifts a week, and if I wanted to work more that would always be on the table.

Best of all, Jacob was supportive of all of it. While I could sense that he was a touch worried about the mother of his child running around the city going from class to work and back again, he was happy to see that I was feeling well enough to live life as I had before.

I had to admit, I was loving my new car – especially the independence it afforded. I'd find myself taking it out for drives all the time, heading up and down the PCH or into the city, taking long drives down Santa Monica Boulevard and into all the places in the LA area that I'd never been able to see.

"You know," Jacob said as we ate dinner in our usual spot on the patio near the pool. "You're treating LA like a place you've never lived before."

"That's because that's kind of the case," I said. "I grew up in Bakersfield, so LA was always this mystical, magical place off in the distance."

"But you all ended up here."

"Yes. I moved for school, Maryann moved for a job, and Corrine moved when Mom finally snagged her first LA guy who paid her way into the city. But since I've never had a car, my world's pretty much just been the area around UCLA."

He smiled. "And now the city's yours."

"I don't know about *that*. But I definitely have more freedom than ever before. And I'm starting to realize just how big this place really is."

That got a laugh out of him. "Yep, LA is most definitely that." After he said the words, he looked away thoughtfully. I could tell that something was on his mind. "You ever been to New York?"

"Jacob, I've never even been out of southern California. Why?"

"This new club that I'm planning for in Vegas...it's something of a trial run. I've done my research and crunched the numbers, and I've got no reason to believe that it's going to do anything but succeed in an enormous way – especially with Archie as the man in charge."

"OK..." I was very curious as to where he was going with this.

"Anyway, that's at least a couple of years in the future, at the soonest, but if I can manage to have two successful clubs in the southwest up and running, I'm going to want to expand as quickly as possible – and I've got my eye on New York."

"Is that right?"

"It is. There'd be plenty of back-and-forth happening while I did all the preliminary work, but the end result would be the two of us living a two-city sort of lifestyle. Well, the three of us, that is. It could be too much, or it could be exciting and fun as hell. Think about it – spending our springs and falls in New York and heading back here during the summer and winter."

The idea was crazy. He was clearly thinking there was a future between us.

I didn't even know what to say to him.

"It's interesting, I'll give you that."

He smiled, as if realizing the implications of his statements. Then Jacob placed his hand on mine.

"Just something to think about – nothing to decide right now. It's all very far into the future."

His easy, calm nature mellowed me out instantly.

"It's just that my world has been so small for so long. I'm just now getting used to how I can drive somewhere and go more than a few dozen miles away from my apartment. New York...I've always wanted to go there, but it's been more of a dream than anything else."

"Well, that's the thing about this new life of yours – you're going to have to get used to a hell of a lot of dreams becoming reality."

I couldn't help but smile. Knowing I was going to be potentially spending my life with this man...it was all so surreal.

"Anyway, as I've already mentioned, I don't want to put too much on you right now. We've still got the baby to worry about, not to mention sorting out the situation with your mother."

The mere mention of Mom made my stomach tighten.

Battling her was becoming exhausting, but impending motherhood shored me up even more.

She would never get her hands on what was rightfully mine. Or my child's.

I was ready to take care of her once and for all. Sunday couldn't come soon enough.

The rest of the week flew by, and when I finished up my shift at Culprit on Sunday, I was actually looking forward to dinner.

"I still can't get over that car," Laura said, the two of us seated on the patio as I took my break. "You're really driving that thing around town, huh?"

I shrugged, glancing over to take in the sight of my BMW SUV looking especially majestic in the gleaming sunlight.

"I mean, I thought it was kind of too much at first. But when you're driving around the city and you see how insane other drivers are, you realize how much you want to be high up and safe. I know it kind of sounds like an old lady thing to care about, but—"

Laura shook her head. "Don't even think of trying to explain. You're a *mom* now. You've got yourself and your kid to worry about."

I glanced down to see that I'd once more placed my hand on my belly – something I did all the time now without thinking since I'd learned I was pregnant.

"As far as I'm concerned," she went on, "you'd be more than entitled to drive around in a tank if you wanted. And I bet Jacob would even buy you one." She grinned. "Seriously, what's it like living with him? I mean, the money has got to be insane."

"I try not to think about it. At first, I thought he was just some guy with a pretty good business sense, somebody that knew how to manage their money. But the other day he sat down with me and told me exactly how much he was worth. He wasn't bragging or anything; I guess he just figured that I needed to be aware of his financial situation."

"And...?" her eyes lit up.

I sighed and shook my head. "Let's just say that you could drop the money I'm getting from my inheritance into his net worth, and you wouldn't even notice it."

"*Woooow,*" she said. "So, we're talking about enough money to where you'd never have to work again in your life, if that's what you wanted."

"I guess. But that's not what I'm going to do. I still want to finish my degree then continue on and get my master's and then my Ph.D. When that's done...who knows?"

"And you've talked to him about this? He's cool with it?"

I grinned. "He'd better be because it's happening no matter what. But yeah, we talked about my plans and he's supportive."

Laura nodded. "Then it sounds like you're in a pretty good situation, lady."

I checked my phone. "Alright – one hour left until the big show tonight. Got to get in the right mindset, you know?"

"Oh, I know. And good luck. You're going to need it."

Laura and I said our goodbyes, and I headed back into the shop to finish my shift. When I was done, I drove back to Malibu to shower and prepare for dinner.

Jacob was in his office, and when I was ready to go, he stepped out in a crisp, white dress shirt, dark blue slacks, and brown oxfords. It was such a simple ensemble, but *damn* did he make it look good.

"Ready to do this?" he asked.

"Ready as I'm going to be."

We took his car, making the drive to Brentwood and arriving a little after six. Mom greeted us at the door, Lila in her arms.

As I greeted Mom, I took special notice of Lila. It was crazy to think that in a matter of months I was going to have a little girl or boy like her. A tiny baby, all of my own.

"You two look dressed up," she said, giving Jacob and me a once over with skeptical eyes.

Jacob fielded this one. "Well, we've got some big news to share with the family. Guess we figured we could dress up a bit for it."

"What kind of news?" Mom asked, handing Lila to me then stepping aside to let us into the house. "Have you two maybe come around on the little issue that we've all been dealing with?"

Jacob and I shared a look. Of course she'd figure the news would have to do with her and not us.

"News?" Maryann asked, she and Corrine looking up from the dining room table where they were both finishing laying out the place settings. "What's going on?"

Lila babbled as I held her, her tiny little hands reaching out trying to grab at my earrings.

"We should probably all sit down," I suggested.

Sam glanced over as he pulled a big, red Dutch oven out of the stove.

"Well, let's do it over dinner," he said. "Got some venison stew going and it just needs to cool off. You two want a beer?"

"Water for me," I answered too quickly. Maryann and Corrine glanced at each other, both of them noticing the speed with which I'd replied.

"Whatever you've got is great," said Jacob.

Sam set the Dutch oven down on the counter and went to the fridge to pull out a pair of beers for himself and Jacob.

"Go ahead and sit, guys," Sam said. "I'll pass everything out."

We took our places at the table, no one saying a word as I handed Lila off to Mom so she could put her in the highchair; Jacob and I sliding into our seats after.

"Well?" Mom asked. "Out with it, already!"

Jacob and I shared a look, one of genuine warmth and affection.

"Jacob and I are having a baby."

You could've heard a pin drop.

CHAPTER 22

JACOB

"You're having a baby?"

It was pretty funny to watch the bomb go off at the table.

Her sisters were thrilled, of course. Their eyes lit up and their screeches nearly broke the crystal.

Naomi, on the other hand, looked like a ghost.

The color had totally drained from her face, and I could almost see her plans falling apart right before her eyes.

Sam was surveying the situation, as if waiting for cues from Naomi on how he was supposed to react. Lila giggled and cooed all the while, totally oblivious to what had just happened.

Maryann and Corrine let out wild screams of excitement, both springing up from the table and rushing over to their sister to throw their arms around her.

"OK, easy!" Delilah laughed as her sisters squeezed her.

"Sorry, sorry!" Corrine gave her sister one last hug before moving back to her seat, Maryann doing the same. Once they were seated, the two sisters shared a look that made it clear they were just waiting for the right moment to start asking all kinds of questions.

Naomi's reaction was more measured. Clearly, she'd been

shocked at first. But once that wore off, the expression that replaced it was more measured, calm, almost blank, even.

It was the expression of a woman who was in the process of changing her plans, figuring out her next angle.

"That's wonderful news, Delilah." Naomi's tone was as calm as her face. "I had no idea you were trying for a baby so soon."

Delilah shrugged. "We weren't, actually, but both of us are very happy it happened. I'm getting so excited."

Naomi nodded. "That's very good. So happy to hear that Lila and the rest of you girls are going to have a little niece or nephew."

Despite her words, her tone was completely emotionless.

Then she flicked her eyes over to me, as if she were trying to get a sense of what was going on in my head. Luckily, I was damn good at keeping my emotions hidden.

Naomi was silent the rest of the dinner. Maryann and Corrine did most of the talking, barraging their sister with questions about names and such.

All the while, Naomi's mouth was set in a line, the corners curled downward slightly. I could sense that she'd gone from shock to scheming in record time.

I was relieved to get out of there when the dinner was over.

"How do you feel about all that?" I asked as we drove back to Malibu. "Did it go as you had hoped or expected?"

"Good." Delilah said the word with a definitive tone. "I was nervous as hell at first, but now that it's all out in the open I'm glad." She turned away from the window, her eyes on me, concern on her face. "You noticed how Mom was, right? I told her and it was like she...I don't know, shut down."

"Oh, I noticed. But you're her daughter; what do you think her reaction was all about?"

I had my theories, but I was eager to hear what Delilah had to say about it.

"She's planning something," she said. "She's always got an angle. I bet you anything that when I told her about the baby, her first thought was how it was going to affect her chances of getting her hands on my money. Then she switched to thinking about how she could play the situation to her advantage."

"And there it is," I said. "I don't want to be too cynical about your mother, but that's the impression I got, too."

"We're going to need to keep an eye on her." Delilah said the words definitively, as if there were no doubt in her mind.

It made me feel terrible for her. I hated that she needed to have such suspicion about her own mother.

We were both tired when we returned to the house. Delilah could barely keep her eyes open as she crossed the threshold.

"Want some tea?" I asked.

She answered by stretching out her long, willowy limbs and yawning.

"It sounds good, but I think I'll be out by the time the water's hot. Thank you though." She stepped over to me and leaned up, planting a kiss on my lips. "And thanks for everything else. I know that dealing with my family's got to be one of the weirdest things you've done, but I really appreciate you being there."

"Hey, you're still paying me to do it, remember?" I winked, and she laughed and rolled her eyes.

"Goodnight, Jacob."

With that, she went up the stairs, my eyes lingering on her perfect ass as she did.

I'd wanted to invite her to my bed since she'd arrived. But between the baby and her school and my work, I hadn't gotten the chance. Plus, I wanted her adjustment to her new home to be as painless as possible.

When I was alone, I poured myself a whiskey and stepped out onto the patio.

The night was on the warmer side – a sign that spring was well on its way. As I sipped, I thought about Naomi. There was no doubt in my mind that she was planning something.

Whatever it was, I would need to be ready.

~

That Friday, Delilah and I had our first spat.

"You can't just tell me not to go! That's not how this works!"

Delilah was in the kitchen of my Malibu place, her face tight with anger.

"I'm not demanding you do anything," I said, trying to keep my voice calm. "I'm simply telling you what I feel is the most reasonable thing to do. You woke up this morning sick again, and now you want to spend the entire day out. It doesn't make any sense to me."

"That's because you're not seeing it from my point of view. You're acting like I'm going out clubbing or something which is the farthest thing from the truth. I'm going to school so I can do my labs for the day. I realize your thing is strip clubs and not education, but I kind of need to do this stuff if I don't want to end up on one of your stages."

She immediately bit her lower lip, glancing aside after she said the words. I could sense she knew that she was out of line.

"Sorry – that was too far. But I feel like you're treating me as if I were some helpless pregnant lady who can't be trusted to leave the house on her own."

"You're putting words in my mouth," I shot back. "I don't think you're helpless at all. What I *do* think is that sometimes you're too damn determined for your own good. You want to go to school, fine. But you need to do some accepting of the situation that you're in – namely that you're pregnant and still having morning sickness."

"I'm well aware of the situation I'm in – I'm the one going through it."

"Then why do I have to explain to you that you're in no condition to spend all day on campus?"

She closed her eyes and clenched her fists in frustration, her body language sending the clear message that she wasn't happy with what I'd just said.

"Listen, I know you're a manager and all, but I'm not one of your employees who you can just tell what to do. I'm my own person with my own life and I don't need you looming over my shoulder deciding for me if I'm fit to leave the house or not. I can't just lay in bed for the next several months. Many women have morning sickness and still live their damn lives."

"I know that you're not one of my employees. But you are somebody that I care about, and you *are* being too stubborn for your own damn good!" After I spoke, I realized that I raised my voice, which was something that I rarely did. Delilah had gotten the better of me, and I understood with that outburst, I'd lost the argument.

"I'm going to school," she said, her voice calm and even. "I'm going to be gone most of the day. Don't wait up."

Without another word, she grabbed her backpack from the counter, slung it over her shoulder, and left the house. I heard the purr of the BMW engine as she started it, and then she was gone.

I sighed, frustration still boiling inside of me.

I wasn't mad at Delilah; I was more frustrated by the situation. So, I did what I did when I had free-floating tension inside of me – I worked out.

After changing, I started with a warmup run along the beach, getting in a good couple of miles before heading back inside and stepping into my personal gym. I put on some rock music, letting it blast through the stereo system as I lifted until I couldn't lift anymore.

I felt better once I'd gotten in a good hour or so, and the shower afterward felt amazing. When I was dressed and ready to start my day, I couldn't help but check my phone to see if any texts or calls from Delilah had come in.

There was nothing.

The morning was nearly over, and I found my thoughts drifting to Cherry Lane.

Friday afternoons meant low-key affairs at the club - I reserved that time for some of my big-name clients who enjoyed wining and dining their guests for whatever reason.

I realized that I hadn't been to the club in a week or so. I made the decision to head out to my place of business and check on things.

I took the long way back to West Hollywood, rolling down the window and enjoying the perfect LA weather. The sun beat down and warmed my face, and I couldn't help but let a smile form on my lips as I drove north on Santa Monica Boulevard.

I arrived at the club a little after one, feeling better as soon as I stepped into the swanky interior. Just as I'd predicted, the place was about a third full, a few of my girls busy bringing drinks to the guests as they sat and chatted quietly in their booths. As I passed, I noticed several of them glancing up at me long enough for a brief nod.

It felt damn good to be there, and part of me wondered if I'd made a mistake in stepping away from the day-to-day operations of Cherry Lane.

There was no thrill like running the place on a busy Friday night, the air crackling with an energy that you couldn't find anywhere else.

I took the elevator to the fourth floor, noticing that my office door was shut. As I approached, I could hear Archie's low voice on the other side.

A small smile on my face, I knocked.

"Come in!"

I opened the door to see him at my desk, his feet propped up, phone in his hand.

His eyes flashed when he saw it was me.

"Alright, that sounds good," he said to the person on the other line. "Boss man's here, so I'll confirm with him and let you know."

With that, Archie hung up the phone and sprang out of his seat, moving with surprising speed for a man his size.

"Boss," he said, the look on his face as if he'd done something wrong. "You're here!"

I chuckled. "You sound surprised."

"Well, I am. I didn't know you were planning on stopping in today."

"Just wanted to swing by and see if anyone needed anything." I glanced at the desk. "You're the man in charge right now. Go ahead and sit."

He shook his head, stepping away from the desk. "Nah, feels weird to be in the big chair when you're here. I'll take it back when you're gone."

I chuckled lightly, amused, but I slid into the seat, the chair as comfortable and familiar as ever.

So, how're things in that *other* life of yours?" Archie asked.

I sat back and told him what had gone down with Delilah that morning.

It felt strange because I was normally the sort of man that kept my feelings to myself when it came to personal matters.

I simply told Archie about the dispute, how she'd left in a huff, and that I'd come to work to distract myself.

"I figured something was up," he said. "Kinda strange that you'd pop in out of nowhere like this."

"Didn't know what else to do. It was either that or go to UCLA and try to hash things out there."

Archie winced as I said that. "Yeah. Don't do that. What you've got here is a...let's call it a classic difference of opinion. Thing about situations like these is that no one's in the wrong, really. You're right for wanting to look out for her, to make sure she doesn't overextend herself, and she's right for wanting to have some semblance of her normal life, of what she's used to."

As always, Archie had laid it out in a way that I couldn't argue with.

"Then what the hell do I do? This relationship shit...I'm hardly experienced."

"Yeah, no kidding. And knowing you this would be the time when you'd decide that the girl was too much trouble and drop her. But...that's not the case here. You like this girl too much."

I wanted to dispute that, tell him that he was wrong, but there was no denying it – I was crazy about her.

"That obvious?"

"Only because I know you so well."

I snorted, shaking my head, and wondering how I'd gotten in so deep, so quickly.

"She came out of nowhere. And just like that..." I snapped my fingers.

"That's how it always goes, J. One minute you're living life, the next you've got a girl you'd do anything for."

A chuckle escaped out of me. "Well, you're definitely right about how I got here. But you're not telling me how to navigate my way out of this."

Archie tended to look away whenever he was deep in thought. He glanced toward the windows overlooking the club. Then he brought his eyes back to me.

"Give her some space. All this was about how she wanted to spend the day on campus, right? Well, let her do that, and don't suffocate her. Trust that she'll get in touch if anything comes up that she needs your help with. And maybe tomorrow you can talk about it without the heat of the moment on top of you."

His words made perfect sense.

"Where the hell did you get to be so damn smart, Arch?"

He grinned. "When you're not a player like someone I know," he nodded toward me, "and you actually take the time to *date* women, you learn a thing or two."

"Makes sense. Now, what the hell do I do with myself in the meantime?"

"Take a look where you are, boss. I think you've got the answer right in front of you."

He was right - again.

I'd made the correct call handing things over to Arch for a while, but tonight, I was the man in charge.

I rose from my seat, stepping over to the window that overlooked the club. I clasped my hands behind my back and gazed down at my domain.

"Let's get ready for a hell of a night."

CHAPTER 23

DELILAH

The first half of the day flew by so quickly that I didn't even have time to think about the fight I'd had with Jacob that morning. Class had started at eight-thirty, the lecture lasting until ten then I had my first lab of the day. It was an intense one, too - an advanced study on prediction patterns according to Mendelian genetics.

I'd been in the zone, so focused that I was able to block out everything outside of the work. Soon enough, it was time to go back to the real world.

The memory of the fight came rushing right back.

I knew it wasn't going to go anywhere.

Laura texted as I stepped out of the UCLA Life Sciences building, and I was happy as hell to see that she wanted to meet up for lunch.

I eagerly agreed, and thirty minutes later the two of us were seated outside, salads from the cafeteria on our laps as we soaked up the sun.

She listened intently as I filled her in and vented all at the same time. When I was done, she looked thoughtfully into the distance in front of her, thinking it all over.

"You've got to talk to him," she said, sticking her fork into a cherry tomato and popping it into her mouth.

"That's what we tried to do this morning. Didn't work out so well."

"No, you didn't talk – you fought. There's a big difference. Talking would mean you sat down with each other and tried to figure out a compromise, to meet each other in the middle. Fighting is just trying to brute force your way into making the other person see your side of things.

I shifted my weight, knowing she was right.

"Don't worry too much about it. And keep in mind that he did what he did because he was trying to look out for you in his own way. So try not to bite his head off too much." She winked, and together the two of us returned our empty trays, talking about the weekend ahead and making plans for lunch and a little shopping the following day.

Laura's next class started before mine, so she took off after we returned our trays and left me alone.

My thoughts, of course, went right back to the fight or discussion or whatever I'd had with Jacob. I realized that Laura had made some good points.

Jacob hadn't asked me not to go to class because he wanted to control me. No, he'd done it because I'd been throwing up that morning and he was worried about my health.

I knew I had good intentions, as well. For the time being, I was going to get my head into the right space, preparing for the conversation with him later that we needed to have.

All of a sudden, I spotted a familiar figure in the distance coming toward me.

"No way," I muttered to myself, taking off my sunglasses to get a better look.

My eyes weren't deceiving me as I watched my mother approaching.

"There you are," she said as she came near, whipping off her

Gucci sunglasses and taking a seat next to me as if we'd had plans to meet. "I've been looking all over this place for you."

I didn't know what to say.

"We need to talk," she said. "And you know about what."

I shook my head, forcing myself to come into the moment, preparing for what was certain to be a battle.

"What...how the hell did you find me here?"

She cocked her head to the side, as if I'd asked the stupidest question imaginable.

"Are you kidding? I know you like to pretend otherwise, but I'm your *mother*. A few phone calls to the biology department and some persuasive words were all I needed to get your schedule. Besides, one of the girls in the biology office spotted you down here having lunch with that Laura friend of yours."

Maybe it had been a silly question. Mom was uncompromising and extremely good at getting what she wanted when she wanted it.

"I don't have the time or the energy for a conversation with you right now, Mom. I've got labs all day and I need to have my head in the right place. And that means I absolutely do *not* want to talk about whatever you've got on your mind."

"Well, I've got news for you, kid. I'm here now, and we're going to talk if I have to follow you around campus and scream in your ear."

Once more I was reminded of the lengths that Mom would go to in order to get what she wanted. I sighed.

"What is it?"

"Tell me the truth. Are you really pregnant?"

"What?" I couldn't believe what I was hearing.

"Are you really pregnant? Or is this thing a lie that you cooked up, so you didn't have to give me any money?"

I said nothing at first, my jaw dropping open and my eyes going wide.

Mom wasn't about to let me stand there speechless. "Well? Give me the straight truth – and don't you try to BS me."

I blinked hard, allowing her question to sink in and giving myself a chance to collect my thoughts.

"Let me get this straight – you're asking if I'm *faking* a pregnancy?"

"I wouldn't put it past you to try anything to get me to stop asking you to help support your family. And what better way to do it than to put on a big show acting like you've got a kid of your own on the way?"

She scoffed and shook her head, as if she'd cracked the case and couldn't believe the truth she'd uncovered. "And you know what else I wouldn't put past you? That you've become a little envious of the spotlight. I've got Lila, a precious little girl as cute as they come, and now that the focus isn't solely on you, you can't *stand* it. Not enough that you're marrying some rich club bigwig. No – you've got to have *all* the attention."

I let out a scoff of my own. "Mom, I know I'm a biology major and not a psychology one, but I'm pretty sure this is a clear-cut case of projection. You're laying out this insane plan and the more you talk, the more it sounds like something *you'd* pull."

Mom narrowed her eyes at me, and I could sense that I'd hit close to the bone.

"I've been doing a lot of thinking about everything that's been going on in your life. And the more I do, the more I realize that there's something very fishy about it all." Her eyes still narrowed, she glanced off into the distance, as if putting more clues together. "You, a girl who hasn't so much as *dated* a man, as far as I know, suddenly shows up with one of the biggest playboys in LA at her side. Seriously, I looked into this guy – I know what he does, and I know how much he's worth."

My heart skipped a beat. It wasn't a surprise to know that Mom had done her research.

"How does that happen, exactly?" she asked. "How does a mousy, school-obsessed girl like you end up with a man who could have any woman in the city he wanted? And then, on top of it all, you just *happen* to get pregnant?" Mom nodded, as if she were now certain with herself. "Something really strange is going on here. And right now, I'm giving you the chance to come clean with it."

"We love each other," I said. "And if you want to act like there's some grand conspiracy going on because that's the lens you view the world through, then so be it. Not like there's anything I can do to talk you out of it. And I *am* pregnant, believe it or not. Jacob and I are thrilled, and I have to say, it's disappointing that my own mother is coming at me like this rather than sharing in our joy."

With a disgusted gasp, she rose from her seat. She didn't wait another moment before turning on her heels and storming off. I kept my eyes on her until she'd melted into the crowd of students and was gone.

The relief was instantaneous, washing over me the second I couldn't see her any longer.

As I caught my breath, a thought occurred to me – specifically, a word I'd used.

Love.

I'd said that I loved him.

The more I considered it, the more I realized it was true.

I shook my head, a small smile on my face at the idea that I'd found the one way to make a complicated situation even more insane than it already was.

CHAPTER 24

JACOB

I was in my office, my eyes on the evening scene below me, a glass of whiskey in my hand, when a knock sounded.

Knowing it was Archie, I called for him to come in.

"Evening, boss." He stepped into my office with a silver laptop tucked under his arm.

"What's up?" I asked as he took a seat in the meeting area in the corner of my office.

Archie placed his laptop on the coffee table and opened it up. I moved over and sat down next to him.

"Finally got some info on Delilah's grandmother."

A smile formed on my face.

Ever since Delilah had told me about her grandmother, and how Delilah's mom had kept them apart, I'd made it a goal to track her down.

"Talk to me." I sipped my whiskey and sat back, eager to hear what he had to say.

"Well, it wasn't easy."

"Naturally. You didn't even have a name to go on. But I was confident you'd be able to pull it off."

"Well, that's appreciated. The crazy part about it is how much effort Naomi went to make sure that her own mother couldn't get in touch with her."

"As in, she'd cut her out of her life?"

"Looks like it. I had to hire a couple of PIs to poke around in Naomi's information to trace birth certificates and all that. Ended up finding Delilah's grandma through a hospital visitation sign-in sheet from ten years ago – the last time that the two spoke. Grandma's name is Helen, by the way."

"Good work Arch. Let's see what you've got."

He nodded, then leaned forward, clicking here and there. Seconds later, a picture of a woman appeared on the laptop screen.

The photo was a candid shot, the woman in the picture attractive and elegant, looking to be in her late sixties. She was seated at an outdoor table at a café, dressed in expensive clothing.

While I couldn't tell the location exactly, it struck me as somewhere in western Europe.

"Don't tell me you have a PI following her around," I said.

Archie chuckled. "Just briefly, to confirm it was her. Don't worry – we're not tailing her."

The more I looked at the picture, the more I could see the family resemblance. She reminded me quite a bit of both Delilah and Naomi.

"We've got all her info – where she lives, what she did for a living. Turns out that she used to be a lawyer, believe it or not. Had her own private practice in New York, sold it to her partners then retired in London."

"So, she's got money."

"You bet."

I didn't know the whole story, but it appeared that whatever had happened between Naomi and her mother, had involved money. But then I was only speculating.

"There's more info, but it's just background stuff." Archie stood up and headed to the bar, pouring himself a little something to drink. "So, now that you have the scoop, what're you going to do, J?"

I sipped my own drink, my eyes on the screen as I let everything I'd just learned wash over me. I remembered there was still the matter of the argument Delilah and I had earlier.

I'd been spending the whole day fighting off the urge to give her a call, knowing that the best thing to do would be to give her a bit of space, like Archie had said.

"Give me the room," I said. "I'm going to give her a call."

"You got it. I'll be nearby if you need anything." With that, Archie threw back the rest of his drink, then set the glass down before heading out.

When I was alone, I pulled up the sheet of information, my eyes going right to Helen's cell phone number. I began a text letting her know that I was a friend of Delilah's, and that I had very happy news about her granddaughter. I finished by telling her that I was available to talk whenever she wanted.

I took another sip of my whiskey and set the phone down. It occurred to me that it was late in London – a little past ten.

I didn't need to consider the matter for too long. My phone buzzed with a text, and I quickly read it.

Who are you? What is this news about my granddaughter?

I wasted no time typing up a response.

I'm sure you have questions. If you're available to speak now, I can answer all of them.

The response came seconds later.

I want to talk now. And I want to see your face, whoever you are.

Perfect.

I can FaceTime ASAP. I'll be waiting for your call.

I didn't need to wait for long. The FaceTime call came moments later, and I transferred it to the big TV in my office.

The woman who answered was more stylish and glamorous than I expected. Her face was slender, her expression no-nonsense, her silver hair in a bob and her eyes a brilliant blue.

The background was a stunning apartment in what appeared to be the Kensington district of London. I could tell because the huge bay windows behind her looked out onto the city, the night skyline shining brightly.

"Alright," she said, her voice American-accented. "Who are you, and why are you messaging me about my granddaughter?"

"Right to the point," I said. "A woman after my own heart."

My compliment didn't have the desired effect. Instead of being flattered, Helen narrowed her eyes as if she'd right then and there decided not to trust me.

I opened my mouth to speak, but she didn't give me a chance.

"Your name," she said. "Let's start with that."

After she spoke, she reached out of frame and lifted a crystalline glass filled with a clear liquid and sipped it, latching her eyes back onto me the second the glass was placed back down.

"Jacob," I said. "Jacob Nichols."

"Alright, Jacob Nichols. Now you can tell me why you texted me, and what's going on with my granddaughter."

My first inclination was to lie, to give her the same story that Delilah and I had told Naomi.

I quickly decided against that. I wanted Helen on our side, and if I hoped to accomplish that, I knew I'd need to tell her the truth.

So, that's what I did. I told her about the fake engagement, and why Delilah had done it. I told her about how I was helping her keep her inheritance away from her mother, and how I'd fallen for Delilah in the process.

As I spoke, Helen regarded me with the same still, narrow-eyed expression, as if she were waiting for the slightest slip-up or inconsistency in my story.

It made me confident in my decision to not lie to her – no doubt she would've spotted any tall tales right away.

"So," she said when I briefly paused. "You've embroiled my granddaughter in a lie."

There was more to come clean about. "It only started as a lie," I tried to defend it. "Now...it's true."

Helen cocked her head to the side. "No speaking in riddles – be plain with me."

"It started out as an arrangement," I continued. "But now...I love her. I love Delilah. And she's pregnant with our child."

Up to that point, Helen had been serious and stoic, grilling me with the force and precision of a veteran detective.

But in that moment, her face softened for the first time since we'd begun our conversation. She cocked her head to the side, as if she hadn't heard me quite right.

"You...she's...pregnant?"

I nodded. "Only a month or so along. But everything we've heard from the doctor has been positive. With any luck, we'll have a beautiful great-grandson or daughter for you to dote on before too long."

Tears formed in Helen's eyes. She quickly wiped them away, and I could tell right then that she wasn't the sort of person to wear her emotions on her sleeve.

"That's wonderful news." She cleared her throat and took another sip of her drink. "And I assume that you're planning on doing the right thing and helping Delilah raise the child?"

"If she'll have me in her life, it'd be an honor." It was strange to hear such words come out of my mouth.

"Good. Well, as you know, things aren't exactly peaceful between Naomi and me. We've had our differences, and she's made it clear that I'm not welcome to visit her children. I've fought with her about it in the past, but my daughter...she can be a vicious one when she wants to be."

"I don't want to step into the middle of your family's affairs, but I believe that the time is right for you to come back into your grand-daughter's lives."

She nodded. "And I assume you have a plan for how to make this happen?"

I did. And I was ready to put it into motion.

CHAPTER 25

DELILAH

I didn't want to speak to anyone after the confrontation with Mom. So, when the school day was done, I fired off a text to Jacob letting him know that I was going to be staying at my old apartment that night.

I knew that the issue between us needed to be addressed, but that night wasn't the time for it.

Jacob's response was a simple: *Understood. Let me know if you need anything.*

I couldn't tell if he was upset or not.

It was a little after nine when I got back to my apartment. A strange feeling came over me when I flicked on the lights.

The place was familiar, but also unfamiliar, as if I hadn't been there in years rather than weeks. Yet, it still felt like home.

I was more than happy to kick off my shoes, toss my backpack on to the floor, and plop on the couch like I so often did just weeks ago.

There was some bottled water still in the fridge, so I cracked one open while I clicked around on Grub Hub to find something to eat.

I settled on Mexican, ordering some tacos and nachos, my

stomach already grumbling as I settled back into the couch and turned on the TV to browse Hulu.

It was nice – a night like I hadn't had in what seemed like a long while.

Damned if I didn't miss Jacob.

As frustrated as I was about the fight - he *had* been totally pigheaded and stubborn - I still cared about him, wanted to be near him. I placed my hand on my belly, knowing there was a little person growing inside of me – *our* little person.

Everything else seemed so small and silly compared to the importance of our baby boy or girl.

The food arrived and I settled in, munching my tacos as I caught up on *Killing Eve*, but I had a hard time paying attention.

My mind kept drifting back to Jacob and the baby and our future together. I was excited and scared at the same time. I couldn't shake the idea that any moment not spent building our life together was a moment wasted.

I ate my food and went to bed, thankfully falling quickly into a deep sleep, waking up a little after eight the next morning.

I was well-rested but antsy, so I threw on some workout clothes and drove down to the beach at Santa Monica. I ran for a good half-hour, coming to a stop at my usual spot by the boardwalk.

My muscles and lungs burned in the best way possible, and I couldn't wait to plop onto the sand and catch my breath.

I sipped my water, watching the waves come in and crash onto the shore.

My eyes were drawn to the families playing on the beach, little kids here and there laughing wildly as they chased the waves and splashed in the water.

As I watched, I did my best to wrap my head around the fact that, in less than a year, I was going to be a mom.

"Nice day for a walk on the beach." A familiar voice spoke behind me. I gasped, turning to face who was speaking – though I knew right away who the voice belonged to.

Jacob was dressed in a pair of off-white linen shorts that hit a few inches above the knee, along with a dark blue Cuban collar shirt opened enough to show off a good portion of his chest. A pair of sharp boat shoes completed the look, along with his usual dark sunglasses. The perfect combination to wear at the beach.

He appeared happy to see me. "You know," I said, "You really shouldn't sneak up on a girl like that. You're liable to get a kick in the balls."

"Well, a guy's got to do what a guy's got to do. You weren't answering your phone."

"Huh?" I reached into the fanny pack I'd brought with me for my run, my phone, keys, and wallet inside. I took out my phone and checked the screen and, sure enough, I'd missed a couple of calls and a text from him.

"I went by your apartment," he said. "And your work. Figured that it was worth a shot to see if you'd come for a run."

"Smart guy," I said with a wink. "Maybe if you decide to get out of the club business you can get into being a detective."

He chuckled as he came over to me. "Mind if I join you?"

"Not at all."

He sat down in the sand next to me. Just having him near felt good, like a missing piece had been put back where it needed to be.

We said nothing for a time, the two of us watching the water, enjoying one another's company.

I knew there was a lot to be said, but I didn't know where to begin.

"You were right." He spoke first, his deep voice carrying over the sounds of the people and the water.

I laughed. "That's a good way to start an apology. But...you were right, too."

"What we have going on...it's not part of my business. You're not an employee that I get to tell what to do. And I know now that if we're going to have something together, it's not going to be on my terms – it's going to be on *our* terms. I care about you, and part of that means I'm going to have to respect your independence."

I didn't know how to respond. He was saying all the right words, and there was no doubt in my mind that he meant them.

"And it's obvious that school's important to you – I respect the hell out of that." He glanced out at the water, as if he weren't sure how to say what he had on his mind. "College was not something that was ever an option. Not how I grew up and where I came from. I was lucky enough to get out of my neighborhood. Thankfully, I used my fists in a smarter way than most and came away with three Olympic gold medals instead of a rap sheet. Then I found my calling with the club scene. It was a lucky break."

He wrapped his arm around my waist, pulling me close.

"Even luckier because it brought you to me."

He moved in and kissed me, and it was a kiss that I was eager to accept. I let his mouth linger on mine, that now familiar taste washing over me, his body solid and warm. We broke the kiss at the same time, as if both of us remembered that we were in public.

"Now," he said. "It sounded like you were about to apologize to *me*." He winked, and I laughed.

"That's because I was. I'm sorry. I appreciate you telling me what you just did, and from my end, I'm going to need to remember that my life isn't just about me anymore. There's you and there's the baby – all of us together. And I know how stubborn I can be. The way you acted was out of care, and I appreciate that."

"Apology accepted." He said the words without the slightest trace of hesitation.

We kissed again, and this time I felt a tension build between my legs.

"I've got an idea," he said, taking his lips from mine.

"Yeah?"

"Let's go back to the house. I think we both need to wash up."

"OK, agreed. Then...after that?"

He grinned. "We'll just have to see what we're in the mood for."

The look on his face left no doubt what he had on his mind.

One more kiss, and we were on our way. The drive back to Malibu seemed to drag on forever. Luckily, the view of the coast was a great distraction from the tightness building between my legs.

We arrived at the mansion and hurried into the house. Jacob and I were on top of each other right away, kissing hard and not wasting any time putting our hands all over one another's bodies.

He moved against me, his hardness pressing against my leg through his shorts. I slipped my hand under the hem of his light shirt, dragging my fingernails over the outlines of his muscles.

Right at the moment he began to take my running shorts off, I froze. Jacob stopped kissing me, moving back, his hands on my hips.

"Something wrong?"

"I wasn't kidding about needing to wash off."

"Then let's go."

Before I had a chance to respond, a sly grin formed on his lips. Jacob bent over, and with an effortless motion, swept me off my feet.

It was so sudden that all I could do was let out a wild cry of excitement as he carried me up the stairs to the third floor. He carried me down the hall and through the double, arched doors at the end. He set me down once we crossed the threshold, and right away I was taken by the room.

The space was huge and open, the entire back wall a clear sheet of glass that led out onto a private balcony complete with a small, well-tended garden. Beyond that, the height of the third floor allowed a sweeping view of the water and sand.

"This way." Jacob peeled off his shirt, pulling it over his head as he made his way to the bathroom, the V-taper of his sculpted upper back enough to make me so freaking wet.

I bit my lip hard, then followed him to the bathroom. The sight on the other side of the threshold was just as impressive.

The bathroom was less of a "bathroom" and more a small, personal spa. There was a large jacuzzi tub in one corner, a huge mirror with three sinks in front of it, and a shower that was big enough to fit a small car.

As impressive as the room was, the man in front of me was what really caught my eye.

Jacob turned to me, the look on his face making it clear how much he wanted me, how much he craved me.

Knowing that was enough to take my desire to the next level. He stepped over to me, placing his hands on my hips, squeezing me just enough to drive me wild.

I stood there, my eyes closed, and my mouth opened just a bit, wordlessly inviting him in for another kiss.

This time, as he kissed me, Jacob slipped his hands down my shorts and over my panties, pulling them both down.

The sensation of being undressed by him drove me mad, the feeling of his rough hands over my skin.

"Now," he said, speaking to me in the stern, commanding tone that so often came out when we made love, the tone that never failed to drive me wild. "Get that gorgeous ass of yours in the shower and let's get you good and clean."

I licked my lips. "Something tells me that we're going to get more dirty than clean in there."

"Maybe. But you'll have to get in to find out."

I was eager to do just that. I started toward the shower and felt the sharp impact of Jacob's hand against my rear, followed by a squeeze.

The swat wasn't hard enough to hurt, of course, but enough to make me gasp, to send a wave of heat rushing through my body. I loved the way he touched me, and every step toward the shower seemed to take an eternity.

When I was inside, I pulled off my shirt and sports bra and tossed them onto the bathroom floor. Jacob did the same with the rest of his clothes, stepping out of his boat shoes and pulling off his shorts and boxer briefs. His cock, thick and long and gorgeous as ever, sprang out to greet me.

Jacob approached, shaking his head as he closed the distance between us.

"What?" I asked. "Something wrong?"

"Nothing's wrong. Just wondering how the hell I went as long as I did without this."

His words washed over me like a warm breeze. There was something about the way he looked at me that never failed to make me feel like the only woman in the world. Jacob stepped over to a futuristic looking control panel and pressed a few buttons. The four nozzles in the shower began to spray out perfect warm streams of water, covering my body and washing away the sweat from my run in a rush of flawless pressure.

"Oh...oh, *wow*..." My voice echoed as I tilted my head back and closed my eyes.

A chuckle sounded through the shower.

"If you want," Jacob said. "I can give you a few minutes."

I opened my eyes and shook my head, coming back into the moment.

"Sorry. Got a little carried away."

He stepped over to me, wrapping his big, thick arms around my waist.

"Now you know how I feel when I look at you."

That was all I needed to hear in order to forget all about the water pressure.

We kissed hard once more, his tongue finding mine as I pressed my naked, wet body against his, my breasts flattening against the muscular rectangle of his chest.

He reached down and swept his hand under my right leg, pulling it up and letting his cock graze against my middle. I shuddered and moaned, melting in his hands.

Jacob placed his hand on the small of my back, moving me across the shower and over to one of the benches against the wall. There, he sat me down and spread my legs, my pussy open and ready for him.

He remained standing, stepping in between my legs, and taking hold of his cock, guiding it down until his head was nestled between my lips.

My breaths were quick and shallow, the anticipation almost too much to bear. Then, with a slow thrust, he moved inside of me.

The position allowed for a perfect view of his cock vanishing into me, all of his inches plunging down, his thickness stretching me out.

When he was fully enveloped, I closed my eyes and savored the feeling of him deep inside of me, pleasure ebbing outward in the way that only he could make me feel. Jacob made me greedy, made me want more.

"You've got no idea how much I've been thinking about this." He pulled back and drove into me again, more pleasure shooting through my body, my breasts shaking from the collision and moans dripping out of me.

"Show me...," I breathed. "Show me what's on been on your mind."

He grinned that sexy grin of his, then leaned in to cover my shoulder and neck in more kisses as he drove into me again, then again.

Each time he moved into me more easily, splitting me in two as I wrapped my legs around his waist. The water splashed down on us, the warm cascade a perfect complement to the pleasure.

We kissed, his taste washing over my tongue, his grunts blending with the rushing of the water. I placed my hands on the perfect muscles of his lower back, feeling them do the work of thrusting.

It wasn't long before the orgasm that had been building finally released, hot, rolling pulses of delight erupting inside of me.

I took in one breath after another when it was over, but the sly expression on Jacob's handsome face let me know he was only just getting started.

However, I had plans of my own. I rose on shaking legs, standing on my tiptoes to kiss him.

"Stay right there," I said. "And let me show you how good you make me feel..."

CHAPTER 26

JACOB

Standing in front of me, water cascading down her perfect body, her hair in thick, honey-brown tendrils on her slender shoulders, Delilah looked like something out of a dream.

Having her before me moments ago with her legs spread, my cock pushing into her over and over...it'd been hard to hold back the orgasm. It was a small price to pay to have more time with her.

"Stay right there," she said. "I want to try something."

That got a laugh out of me. "You sound like you're about to do a science experiment."

"Well, it's something I've never done before. So, in a way, it *is* like an experiment."

I'd almost forgotten that Delilah was inexperienced.

"Let's see what you've got in mind."

She flashed me a sly, sexy little smile.

"Sure. Just...tell me if I'm doing anything wrong."

I was confused by her words, but before I had a chance to wonder for too long what she was talking about, Delilah dropped to her knees in front of me.

She was eye level with my cock, and regarded it with an expression of curiosity, as if it were a piece of machinery that was too complicated for her to understand.

I decided to help her along.

"Take it into your hand," I said. "Start stroking."

She nodded, then followed my suggestion. Delilah wrapped her slim fingers around the thickness of my manhood, a tingle of pleasure following her touch. Then she began moving her hand back and forth, coaxing more sensations of ecstasy out of me.

"It's big," she said. "I don't know how I'm going to fit all of that into my mouth."

"You don't need to fit all of it. Just the end. Then do the rest with your hand."

Keeping her eyes on mine, she gave another nod, this one slower than the last. With a bit of hesitation, she leaned forward and placed her lips on the end of my cock, kissing it gently. That little bit of sensation was enough to make me weak in the knees.

"Like that?"

"Like that."

She covered my head in kisses and licks, glancing up at me with those big beautiful blue eyes as she moved up and down my length. The sight of her working my cock was enough to drive me insane.

Despite it being the first time she'd pleased a man like this, she seemed to know exactly what to do. Or, maybe, it was her inexperience that was turning me on so damn much.

She slowly took more and more of my length into the wet warmth of her mouth. She formed a tight seal with her lips, pushing down as she took as many inches of me into her as she could. When she'd reached her limit, her mouth stretching around my thickness, she went back up.

"Just like that. Keep going back and forth."

Soon she was in a steady rhythm of bobbing her head up and down, her lips firmly wrapped around me, sucking me deeper into her mouth again and again, her fingers stroking the length of my shaft.

I closed my eyes and let my head hang back as I fixated on the pleasure, focused on the sensation of her lips and the wet, sucking sounds.

It wasn't long before I wanted more. I gently guided her off my cock, the end of my manhood falling out of her mouth.

"Stand up," I commanded.

She obeyed, rising to her feet, and putting her gorgeous, tight body on full display once more.

"Was that not good?"

I shook my head. "That's not it at all. It was *too* good."

Delilah smiled, pleased to hear a positive review of her work. "Then you should've let me finish. I would've loved to taste you."

Hearing her say those words brought my arousal damn near to the brink of what I could stand.

"As much as I'd love to watch you drink every last drop," I said. "I want something different."

"Different?"

"That's right." I pointed to the wall ahead of us. "Stand there. And put your palms against the wall."

She regarded me with an expression of curiosity, but then did as she was told. Delilah turned and moved toward the wall, smiling over her shoulder, and swinging her hips playfully from side to side. For a woman so inexperienced, she sure was a quick learner on how to drive a man wild.

Delilah placed her palms on the wall, sticking her ass out. The view was perfect, her round ass like a fruit waiting to be plucked, her pussy glinting between her ripe thighs.

I stepped over to her and placed my hands on her hips. Then I pulled her back hard, a gasp sounding from her mouth as I bent her over.

Her ass right in front of me, I took hold of my cock and placed it at her opening. With a push, I entered her. She moaned, pressing her ass against my body as I glided the last few inches inside.

I pulled back and drove hard.

"Oh *God!*" The thrust must've been more intense than she'd expected. For a moment, I worried that I might've hurt her, but when she glanced back with a smile, I knew that wasn't the case.

I placed my hands on her tantalizing curvy hips, her palms pressed against the wall as I pulled back and thrust my cock into her. Her ass shook from the collision of my body against hers, Delilah turning her head but closing her eyes as more moans shot from her mouth.

I reached forward underneath her, cupping her tits, her nipples grazing against my palm and going hard from my touch.

"Please!" she shouted. "Just like that. Don't stop. Jacob, I'm going to..."

She trailed off, unable to finish the words, moans and sighs sounding instead. Her pussy clenched as she came, gripping me tighter than it already was.

Watching her come in front of me was more than I could take. I released, my cock throbbing inside of her as I shot my load deep. She groaned, pushing her ass against me as if she wanted to make sure every last drop was inside.

The sensation of the orgasm almost too much to bear, I groaned and leaned forward, pressing my hand against the stone wall of the shower, using it to keep myself up.

Neither of us said a word for a time, my chest expanding and contracting as I took in one much needed breath after another.

Delilah turned once more, a satisfied smile on her face.

"Now," she said. "How about we actually get clean?"

We finished in the shower, taking our time, making sure each little bit of one another had been attended to. When we were done, the two of us threw on some fuzzy white robes and went into the bedroom, collapsing on the bed and into one another's arms.

The way I felt with her in those moments...there were no words.

I thought about the conversation with Helen, and how I was going to have to tell Delilah sooner or later that I'd spoken with her grandmother. But not then. I only wanted to savor the unexplainable feelings I was experiencing.

"Alright," she said. "There's something on your mind. What's up?"

Damn. She was nothing if not perceptive. I hated to lie to her, but at the same time, I wanted to keep the news of her grandmother a secret. It was a surprise, after all... sort of.

Not to mention the little fact that I had no idea just how Helen was going to process all that she'd learned. I felt like I'd gotten through to her, but for all I knew she might just decide the drama was too much and stay in London.

So, for the time being, I had to lie.

"Just thinking about what we might do for your birthday. It's this next Saturday, after all."

That got a smile out of her. "Yeah? And what did you have in mind?"

"Here's what I'm thinking. First, we start at the beach. I know some people in the city that I can work with to get a big chunk of the beach at Santa Monica cleared off. We can start the party there, enjoy the weather and watch the sun set over the water."

"Yeah?"

"Yeah. Then, when the sun's down, we reserve the club for a night, throw you the biggest party imaginable."

"Complete with strippers?" she asked with a cheeky grin. "My favorite."

I laughed. "We can hold off on the strippers for one night. Anyway, we'll plan a big party at the club. I can put the word out, let my friends in Hollywood and the recording industry know that it's *the* party of the weekend. Once that news spreads, you're going to see so many stars it's going to be like looking up at the night sky. And they'll all be there for you."

She smiled slightly, looking away. I could tell that something was now on *her* mind.

"What's up?" I asked.

"That sounds amazing. Not going to lie. And it's insanely cool of you to want to go to that much effort for me. I really do appreciate it."

"But..."

"*But* I don't want to sound ungrateful, but I'm really not a huge party person. And especially not this year after all the drama, you know? I wouldn't put it past my mom to try and ruin things somehow if she got wind that I was trying to do something fun for my birthday."

She had a point. Maybe it'd be out of jealousy, maybe out of a simple desire to cause drama – but there was a damn good chance Naomi would try to wreck things.

I wrapped my arm around her, holding Delilah close. She responded by draping her leg over mine, her bare thigh on full display. The sight was enough to make my cock stiffen, letting me know I was ready for more.

I pushed those urges aside, wanting to devote my full attention to what was on Delilah's mind.

"Alright, fair enough. Is there something you'd rather do instead?"

She pursed her lips, as if she didn't want to say it.

"I mean, yeah. But you might think it's boring."

"Try me."

She sat up, turning her attention to the view outside my room's glass walls.

"Well, as far as I see it, you've got a perfectly good beach back here. Santa Monica's great, don't get me wrong. But I'm thinking something a little more low-key might be nice."

"I can do low-key. Plenty of privacy for it."

"How about this – we stay in, make some food, have some drinks outside on the beach. Maybe Laura can come, along with my sisters.

And you could invite a friend or two if you didn't want to feel outnumbered."

Archie came to mind. I'd have to see if he was in the mood.

"That could be nice. We'd have a quiet night here."

She smiled, leaning in, and planting a kiss on my lips.

"Then we could save our energy for the *real* celebration later that night."

As if she were reading my mind, Delilah reached down and wrapped her fingers around my cock.

"Speaking of which, what do you say to a little more practice?"

I grinned, loving the feeling of her fingertips on my hardness.

"Very interested. And I think we ought to, ah, up the intensity of our lessons."

"Good," she said as she moved her body down. "Because you'll find that I'm a *very* diligent little student..."

CHAPTER 27

DELILAH

After the second, er, technically *third* round with Jacob, I wasn't sure if I had it in me to even walk. I lay on the bed like a starfish, my arms and legs spread out and my skin glistening with sweat.

Between the view in front of me beyond the glass wall and the man with a godlike body to my right, I was perfectly content to simply lie there and take in the sights.

However, there was still the matter of Mom. If she'd had it in her to come all the way to school and mess with me there, I had no doubt she was willing to take it to the next level – whatever that might be.

"You alright over there?" Jacob's low, calm voice stopped my mind from racing, like it always did.

He was seated on the edge of the bed, and he turned to place his hand on my belly, regarding it with a small, warm smile before turning his attention back to me.

"Yeah. Sorry. Just got a million things on my mind."

"I don't doubt it. But whatever they are, they can wait. It's Saturday, and we've got the whole day ahead of us to do whatever we want.

We can go somewhere, or if you want to bum around, we can do that."

A day in LA with Jacob sounded heavenly. Then again, so did a lazy afternoon indoors, hanging out on the couch in my pajamas and catching up on some TV, with maybe a dip in the pool to break things up.

"That's something I'm going to need to think about," I said. "In the meantime, I'm going to hop in the shower one more time. That fun we just had was like another workout."

He smirked. "You got it. Take your time in there, relax."

With that, he winked as he got up, reaching around, and giving my ass a squeeze. I laughed, playfully swatting his hand away.

When he was gone, I took a moment to watch the waves come in, the scene so peaceful and quiet and perfect.

I realized that I was getting spoiled. Not with the house and the car, but with how Jacob made me feel. I'd been worried about my impending motherhood, and there was still some lingering apprehension and fear, but Jacob was so damn good at making my worries melt away.

When I was ready, I stepped into the shower, the walls and floor still wet from before.

I followed Jacob's instructions from earlier and used the voice activated commands to turn on the showerheads. I moved into the water streams that hit me from all angles.

When I was done, I threw a towel around me and stepped out into the bedroom. My phone was there, and sure enough there were texts waiting for me – both from the group chat I was in with my sisters. I picked up the phone and swiped to bring the chat on screen.

Maryann: Hey, Des. What happened with you and Mom yesterday?

Corrine: Yeah, she's been sulking and when I tried to ask her what was up, she was just like, 'ask your sister.'

It was clear that Mom wasn't happy about how her confrontation with me at school had gone down. Maybe she'd hoped that by confronting me on my own turf would scare me into going along with whatever she wanted.

I considered my response and typed it up.

She came to campus and tried to spook me there. I told her to leave me alone. Guess she's taking it out on you guys.

I didn't have to wait long for their replies.

Corrine: Figures she'd be pissed about you again. It's like the closer we get to your birthday the more insane she's acting about getting to your money.

A few emojis with the angry face puffing steam out of its nostrils followed.

Maryann: Please tell me you're not going to crack. I'm worried about you, of course, but you know that if she manages to get at your money it's only a matter of time before she comes for Corrine and tries to get at me again.

I grinned as I typed my response.

Not a chance in hell. And I'm going to give Mom as few chances to work her BS on me as possible. That means no dinner at her place tomorrow.

Maryann: Good call. You've got a little more than a week until you get access to the trust. Best thing to do is minimize your contact with Mom until then.

Corrine: Speaking of which...what about your bday?

Her text was followed up by a bunch of different party-related emojis.

You have to do something cool and exciting!

I sat on the edge of the bed, typing up the fun, chill evening I had in mind. Jacob stepped into the room.

"Made a little lunch if you're hungry," he said.

I sent the text to my sisters, and a thought occurred to me.

"Mind coming over here and standing by the window? I want to take a selfie."

"A selfie?"

"Yeah. I'm chatting with my sisters now, and I kind of want to make them a little jealous."

He laughed. "Sure."

I guided him over to the window, making sure that both of us and the amazing view were in the shot. I took the picture, planting a kiss on Jacob's cheek after, then wasted not a second sending the pic to my sisters.

They expressed their good-natured envy in their own ways, Maryann giving me the business through words and Corrine with some strategically used poop emojis.

A big smile on my face, I showed the texts to Jacob. He let out a sharp laugh and rolled his eyes, and in that moment, I realized that someone a decade and a half older than me might not be quite as amused by poop emojis as I was.

"Come on," he said. "Throw some clothes on." After he said the words, a sly smile formed on his lips. "Now, there's something I never thought I'd say to you."

I laughed. "Well, what's the occasion?"

"I decided how we're going to spend the day. Instead of choosing between a day in or a day out, we're going to do both."

"I'm intrigued."

"I couldn't help but notice that your suitcase was a little light, and that you haven't brought that much clothing over from your place."

He was right. I'd managed to cram just about everything I wore on a regular basis into my big suitcase.

"Well, when you're a full-time student *and* have a job, that doesn't leave much time or money for nice clothes. Besides, I'm good with a pair of leggings and a UCLA hoodie most days."

"I'm sure you are. But that doesn't mean you shouldn't have options."

"What kind of options?"

"The kind you find on Rodeo Drive."

While I wasn't the most materialistic person in the world, I had to admit that getting a chance to do some shopping at *the* place for clothes was more than a little enticing.

"That could be nice."

"It will be. We'll do some shopping, grab a little something to eat after. Then we can come back home and have a nice, quiet evening in, maybe split some sparkling cider by the pool."

It sounded heavenly.

"I'm in."

He reached out his hand for me to take.

"Then let's get moving – I don't want to waste a minute."

CHAPTER 28

JACOB

The day was wonderful. After spending the afternoon shopping, we stopped at Mirame, one of my favorite restaurants in the city, for some amazing seafood. After that, we headed home where we enjoyed a post-outing dip in the pool.

Then, it was off to the bedroom where we got down to what had been on both of our minds since the last time we'd been in bed together.

When I woke up the next morning, I laid there for a time, Delilah curled up against me as she often did during her sleep. As the morning light poured over us through the glass, as the waves lapped onto the shore in the distance, as Delilah's chest rose and fell with each breath, I took the time to savor it, to commit every detail to memory.

I knew it was impossible, but I didn't want to forget a moment.

Delilah awoke after a time, opening her sleepy eyes and looking up at me, a smile spreading across her lovely face.

"Morning," I said.

"Morning."

She moved up a little, slipping my arm over her shoulders and resting her head on my chest.

"I had a weird dream," she said. "Very intense."

"Is that right? A good dream or bad?"

She furrowed her brow, giving the matter some thought.

"Good. Yeah, it was good. There was this big group of us all together, you and me and my sisters and even my mom. I don't know what was going on, exactly, but there was no tension between us. It was happy."

"Sounds like a good dream to me."

She smiled. "Yeah. And the weirdest part was that your parents were there."

"What?" Her words took me totally by surprise.

"Yeah, your parents. And it's weird because I've never met them before."

I tensed the way I always did when the subject of my parents came up. At first, she was confused by my reaction. The confusion quickly changed to realization, however.

"Oh, that was so dumb of me. You said your parents were gone." She bit her lip, and I could tell she was quite upset at what she'd said.

While it pained me to have my parents brought up, I pushed those feelings aside. Delilah had brought them up in an innocent way, and she didn't need to feel bad about it.

"It's fine. It happened a long time ago."

She shook her head. "That's not an excuse. I shouldn't have been so clumsy."

I placed my hand underneath her chin, tilting her face up and responding to her concern with a kiss. Her lips lingered on mine, the kiss having the effect of melting the tension from both of us.

"It's OK," I said, taking my lips from hers. "I've come to terms with it."

"Alright. I'll make sure to never bring it up again."

That wasn't what I wanted either. I placed my hand on the small of her back and gave the matter some thought.

"You don't have to do that. I don't want you feeling like you need to walk on eggshells around me."

She wasted no time placing her hand on my wrist, raising her head up to look at me as she did so.

"Seriously, you don't have to tell me. I didn't mean to pry or pressure you."

Though I appreciated her words, I blew past them. If I told anyone anything about myself, it was because I wanted to, not because I felt pressure.

"We're going to be having a child together," I said. "It's only fair you know about my family."

Delilah said nothing, letting me speak.

"There's not much of a story, I'm afraid. My mother and father were, let's say, both from hard upbringings. My father worked as a bartender, and taught some boxing lessons on the side, passing on the skills he'd learned during his time in the Navy. My mother took care of the home and worked odd jobs where she could, mostly housekeeping services for the wealthy – for people who owned homes like this."

As I spoke, I realized that I hadn't talked about my parents in a long, long time. Speaking about them brought up memories, brought up their faces. It was difficult.

Delilah watched me speak with sympathetic eyes, wordlessly letting me know that she was listening carefully to every word. It meant a lot – surprisingly so.

"One night, when I was eight, after my father finished his afternoon shift at the bar, he went to pick up my mother from one of her jobs. He'd left the house telling me that he'd be back in just a few minutes, that we were all going to go out to one of our favorite places for burgers and milkshakes. Our neighbor was there to keep an eye on me, and I remember not even bothering to take off my jacket, since Mom and Dad would be right back.

"One hour passed, then another. A little after eight o'clock, a police car arrived and when I laid eyes on it, I knew somehow that something was very, very wrong."

I clenched my jaw, my stomach tightening as I told the story. Delilah continued to say nothing, her attention on me and her eyes wide with sympathy and understanding.

"It had all happened in a few seconds – that's what the cops told me, at least. After my father had picked up my mother, he'd gone back to the bar to get something he'd forgotten. When pulling out of the parking lot, a drunk driver - someone who'd been drinking at his bar - had whipped around the corner and slammed into them. They were gone by the time the ambulance had arrived."

Delilah took my hand and squeezed it hard. "I'm so sorry."

"Thank you." I brought in a full breath, giving myself a moment to continue. "It was all so surreal – that's what I remember the most. The funeral was closed casket, very modest. The next month or so passed in a kind of strange daze. It took me a while to even begin processing it. And by the time I'd finally allowed myself to grieve, that's when I learned that I didn't have a single family member who wanted me. Instead, I was to be put in the foster system, moving from house to house until I was finally old enough to join the Navy like my father. And like him, I took up boxing."

She smiled slightly. "And then the Olympics?"

I chuckled, that time in my life seeming like a million years ago. I smiled, too – those were good memories.

"Turns out I had a knack for fighting – just like my old man did. And at that age, I was full of enough piss and vinegar that boxing served as a good outlet for all that was going on inside of me. When I was done with my time in the Navy, I moved to LA and got involved in the local boxing scene. Spent about a year working my way up, never lost a match."

"Wasn't long before I was scouted for the US Olympic team. Not like I had anything better going on, so I joined up, trained even harder, and made it to Beijing. Won gold there, then came back to LA."

She laughed. "You say it so easily, that you won the gold, with the same tone you'd use when talking about what you got at the store that day."

That got another smile out of me. "Well, it was a blur of training hard. I barely remember knocking out the Irish guy I fought for the gold. He went down with a hook, then before I knew it, I was getting a gold medal wrapped around my neck. It all felt pretty unreal, really."

"Then what?"

"I came back to LA, my bank account full with some prize money and a little more from a few sponsorships. But I wasn't interested in money – not yet. I was hungry for the fight. So, I went back into local circuits and moonlighted as a bouncer at a few clubs here and there. Wasn't long before I worked my way up to head of security at Cherry Lane. Well, it wasn't called Cherry Lane back then, but you get the idea."

I ran my hand through my hair. I realized it was the first time I'd ever sat down and told my life story to anyone. Part of me wondered if I was boring Delilah. If I was, her face told a different story.

I went on.

"While I worked security, I learned the ins and outs of the place from the owner, a man named DeWitt. Once he saw my potential, my eagerness to learn, he wasted no time taking me under his wing. 2012 rolled around, and Team USA wanted me to go to the London Olympics to box again. DeWitt told me that when I came back, he was ready to begin the process of handing things over to me. I left, I won again, and when I came back, he kept his word and let me run the show."

"Then there was a third gold medal," she said with a smile. "Little detail you're leaving out."

I laughed. "Yeah, there was the third. That came after I'd been running the show in all ways but name. I'd made some good money off my investments, and when the team came calling again, asking if I wanted to start training for Rio, part of me thought that taking some more punches to the head was the last thing I wanted to do. I was now a businessman, after all."

"But DeWitt told me to do it, said that I'd regret it like hell if I didn't get my glory while I was young enough. Not only that, but he said if I brought home the gold one more time he'd retire and leave the club to me entirely. So, I did. I trained hard for months, then went to Rio."

"And you won the gold again."

I grinned – couldn't help it; I was proud as hell when I'd brought home that medal.

"Sure did. I pulled a KO against a kid nearly a decade younger than me, some hothead out of Germany. But I was done, decided to go out on top. When I came back, two things happened – DeWitt handed the club over. Then he told me he was dying of cancer."

Delilah's eyes turned soft, caring. It was as if there were no bounds to her empathy.

"He declined quickly. DeWitt was a stubborn old bastard, the kind of guy who'd rather go out on his terms instead of rolling the dice with treatment. The day he died, he told me that the club was mine, and that he was proud of me."

She smiled, squeezing my hand.

"And that was that. I was officially the man in charge. I renamed the club 'Cherry Lane,' focused on the highest-end clientele I could and turned the place from one of the best clubs in the city to one of the best in the world." I swept my hand out toward the bedroom. "My mom cleaned houses like this. So, when I took over the club, my success confirmed, I bought this place. She might never have been able to live in a home like this, but she's alive in spirit."

That was it – that was my story. When I was done, I felt strange, like a weight had been lifted from me.

More than that, I felt closer to Delilah in a way I hadn't with anyone else.

"Thanks for telling me," she said with a warm smile. "I'm sure your mom and dad would be so proud of you."

Delilah moved up to kiss me, her body, and lips warm against mine. Together, we laid in bed and watched the waves come in on the shore in the distance.

I realized there was no doubt in my mind that I loved this woman like mad.

Shit.

CHAPTER 29

DELILAH

"I'm not ready."

Jacob let out an amused snort at my words. He was always good at reacting to my occasional panic with just the right amount of irreverence.

As I sat in front of my computer, reading the email from my mom, an email she'd sent on the morning of my birthday, I couldn't help but feel a surge of panic.

"You're ready. It's Saturday, and you've got forty-eight hours, less than that, actually, until we go to the bank and you sign all the paperwork. Once you do that, we'll meet with the accountant and get everything sorted out. By the end of the day, you'll have your money good and secured where your mom can't get to it."

He was right, and his words did mellow my anxiety out a bit.

There was still the matter of the email on the screen in front of me.

"You need to read this," I said. "Look at what she said to me on my birthday."

Without a word, his coffee mug in hand, Jacob stepped over to where I sat at the kitchen bar. I moved over, letting him lean in and get a good look at the words on the screen.

The first paragraph was pure guilt, Mom laying it on thick and telling me all about how much she suffered and slaved back when my sisters and I were girls, how she'd sacrificed everything to make sure we had whatever we needed.

It was bullshit, plain and simple. Mom had always put herself first, making sure the liquor cabinet was stocked and that there was a new man in her bed before ever thinking about what we needed.

Jacob let out a chuckle.

"I may have gotten lucky with my parents," he said. "I don't know what it's like to have a mom like this. But I can spot a manipulator from a mile away."

I squeezed his arm, happy that he was on my side. He kissed me on the cheek before turning his attention back to the email.

The second paragraph was about all the things she'd do with the money, how having the security would allow her to make sure Lila had everything she needed. I wasn't just helping her, she said, I was helping my sister. And I didn't want to put my own sister's future at risk, did I?

"She's shameless," he said. "Totally shameless."

"It gets worse."

He kept reading, his eyes moving over the last paragraph, where Mom explained how if I wasn't willing to help my own family out, then it was only right that I didn't get to be a part of the family.

What did that mean in plain terms? It meant that if I didn't want to give Mom any of my money, then I shouldn't expect to see Lila.

"Despicable," Jacob said. "Absolutely disgusting that a mother would use her own children against each other like that."

There was real venom in his words. It made sense now that I knew about his past, how his own parents had been taken from him.

The last bit of the email stated that she expected me to come to dinner tomorrow. If I didn't, then that would be taken as me not wanting to help her, which meant that I wouldn't be seeing Lila any time soon.

"I don't know what to do," I said. "The idea of her never letting me see Lila..."

He put his big hand on my shoulder, the gesture bringing a wave of comfort that washed over me.

"You can't let her win. Let me tell you this – when you give someone like her what they want, they don't stop there. If you give her ten thousand dollars, she's going to be coming back for twenty thousand a few months down the road."

"But Lila..."

He looked away, and I could sense that he was trying to figure that out, too.

"We'll solve it somehow." His tone was one of total certainty.

"And she says that she's expecting us at dinner. Should we skip it?"

He shook his head. "No. We go, and we see what she's got up her sleeve. If she brings the heat, I'll be there for you. Worst case, we leave."

Jacob's jaw worked, and I could tell that the notion of Mom using Lila as a tool like that didn't sit well with him in the slightest.

"There's more to this manipulation," he said. "Your mom knows that it's your birthday – and your twenty-first at that. She sent this knowing that the email would darken what was supposed to be a happy day for you."

He was right. I'd woken up that morning feeling happy and excited about the day ahead. But after reading her email, all I could think about was my baby sister.

"We're not going to let her ruin it," he stated. "We're going to have a great time tonight, OK?"

I smiled. "OK."

"We've got your sisters and Laura coming over this afternoon, along with Archie. And I made reservations for tonight at the Factory

Kitchen. I know you said you wanted a quiet night in, and we can still do that. But I figured I'd give you the option."

"That sounds perfect. We can do a nice afternoon out, then a quiet night in. Or not so quiet, maybe." I grinned, and he wasted no time moving in for a kiss.

"Then let's not wait another second," he said. "And get right to the fun."

After a walk on the beach to clear our heads, we came back just in time for Laura and my sisters to arrive for lunch. Laura had met my sisters plenty of times before, all of them letting out excited screams when they saw one another.

Maryann treated us to lunch, bringing over some sandwiches and salads from a deli near her place. We had a fun afternoon in the pool soaking up the sun and relaxing in the water.

Archie showed up, and the girls and I had a great time getting to know the handsome Irishman. I wasn't sure, but I could've sworn that I'd seen Laura and him flirting.

After the dip in the pool, it was time to get ready for the evening ahead. Laura and my sisters and I used my bedroom to change, and the subject of Mom came up. Corrine and Maryann pressed a bit, wanting to know if Mom had been in touch with me on my birthday.

"Yeah," I said, the tension from before returning to my belly. "She's been in touch, alright."

I told them about the email, about the ultimatum. Needless to say, it didn't go over well.

"That's not right," Laura said, her eyes flashing with anger. "It's insane that a mother would use a sibling like that to try to get at your money. I don't want to step out of line here, but there's something wrong with that woman."

"You're not going to get any argument from any of us," Maryann said as she dropped her dress over her body. "We've all been wondering what she was going to pull in these last few days to try and get what she wanted. It's disgusting, but it's not surprising."

"What are you going to do?" Corrine asked, her big blue eyes wide with concern. "The idea of you not being able to see Lila is horrible."

I took a moment to consider my answer. Everything was riding on how the next few days panned out.

"I'm not sure. But I've got to do something. If I don't stand up to her, then it's only a matter of time before she starts putting the pressure on you, Corrine."

Corrine, innocent and petite, clasped her arms over her chest as if protecting herself.

Maryann spoke up. "Mom must be thinking that if she can get you to give in, then it's only a matter of time before we do, too." She sighed, shaking her head. "Lila wasn't around for Mom to threaten me like this. I don't know what I would've done if she'd laid out this kind of ultimatum."

Silence fell over the four of us. Laura, positive as ever, suddenly broke out into a big smile.

"You've got this," she said. "All of you. Sure, having your baby sister used as a bargaining chip isn't exactly a situation anyone's ready for, but I'm certain you all will figure it out. And if there's anything I can do, just say it."

I couldn't help but smile. Knowing I had my best friend, my sisters and Jacob all on my side went a hell of a long way in making me feel better.

"I'm going to go see if Jacob's almost ready," I said. "You guys finish up."

The girls all had the same look of concern on their faces as I left, as if none of them knew quite what to say. I was glad for their help, of course, but something told me this was a problem that I was going to have to figure out how to solve on my own.

I left the bedroom, passing Archie coming down the stairs on my way to the third floor.

"Cute dress," he said with a friendly smile.

"Thanks." I smiled right back, loving the contrast of a compliment like that coming out of a hulking Irishman.

"You seen Laura anywhere? I, ah, wanted to ask her something."

I held back my grin, knowing exactly what was going on.

"She's changing with my sisters. But she'll be out soon."

"Grand."

I went up the rest of the way to Jacob's room. The door was open a crack, so I went ahead and pushed it open, then stepped inside.

I wasn't at all prepared for what I saw.

Jacob was standing in front of his bed, a set of lacy, pink lingerie held out in front of him. He looked it over, checking out the back and front, along with feeling the texture.

"I'm sorry," I said, a smirk on my face. "Did I walk in on you trying something on?"

He turned slowly, not surprised in the slightest. Jacob chuckled as he looked at me.

"You know I can't leave the house unless I've got something sexy on underneath."

Hearing him say those words in his usual dry, sardonic tone was enough to get a laugh out of me.

"Come over here," he said, his words a command.

I did as he asked, making my way across the room and over to his side. Jacob looked me up and down, taking in the sight of me in my dress.

"You look amazing." He shook his head the way he usually did whenever he looked at me, as if he couldn't believe what he was seeing.

Tingles spread outward from between my legs.

"Thanks."

I bit my lower lip, the sexual tension building in the air by the moment.

"Seriously, though," I said. "What's with the lingerie?"

"Birthday gift. But it was supposed to be a surprise. Didn't count on someone coming into my room without knocking." His lip curled in one corner, and I could tell he was teasing.

My eyes lingered on the lingerie. I imagined myself wearing it, imagined his hands on me as I stood wearing nothing but the skimpy bra and panties.

Just the thought of his touch moving over my skin was enough to turn me on like crazy.

"Well, let me make it up to you."

Before he could ask what I meant, I snatched the set out of his hands and headed off to the bathroom, throwing a smile over my shoulder as I did. He regarded me with an expression of amusement. Once in the bathroom, I slipped out of my dress and took off the bra and panties I'd been wearing, tossing them aside.

I slipped on the new lingerie, the fabric hugging my body perfectly. I was hardly the vain type, but as I looked at myself in the mirror I felt like a damn supermodel.

A pleased grin on my face, I threw the dress over my arm and stepped back into my heels before leaving the bathroom.

Jacob's eyes flashed wide as he took in the sight of me. His hungry gaze moved up and down my body, and I found myself growing more and more turned on with every step I took closer to him.

When I was near, he placed his hands on my hips and brought me close, his cock hard through his slacks.

Without a word, he kissed me slowly and deeply, my body pressing against his, my chest taking in slow breaths. I lost myself in the kiss for a moment, but then pulled my lips away.

"I take it that means you like it."

"I like it," he said. "But it's going to be a damn shame when I rip if off you later tonight."

The way he looked at me with those dark green eyes, the way he spoke, made me want to put the party on hold for a little while. Instead, I traced the outline of his cock through his pants.

"We'll have to see if you're on your best behavior tonight."

He grinned. "Maybe during dinner. But after that, you're not going to see anything close to me behaving."

I couldn't resist kissing him one more time before he slipped the dress from my hands.

"Now, let me help you get this on," he said. "We've got a lot to celebrate tonight before I take it back off."

CHAPTER 30

JACOB

The evening spent celebrating with Delilah and everyone else was the first time in a long time that I'd actually had genuine *fun*. It wasn't just being amused by seeing the others enjoying themselves – I, more than once, found myself letting loose and laughing along with the rest of the group.

The dinner at the Factory Kitchen was perfect, with plenty of drinks and pasta to go around. Every time I glanced over at Delilah, the woman looking like something out of a dream, all I could think about was what I wanted to do with her that night after all the guests had gone home.

"Alright!" Laura said, clasping her hands together. "You ask me, it's time to get to cake and presents."

The restaurant was bustling, every table packed, servers clad in black buzzing around us.

"Yeah," Archie said. "I could sure as hell go for some cake."

He waved at the manager, the woman nodding back to him as if they had some sort of understanding.

"What's going on?" Delilah asked.

"I know some people have a problem with the 'bringing out all the servers to sing happy birthday' thing, but if you ask me, it's one of the most charming traditions you Yanks have. So..."

Without another word, a group of servers emerged from the kitchen, the manager leading the way and carrying a big, cream-colored cake.

"Oh, no!" Delilah's cheeks went red as she covered her face with her hands.

The group came over to the table, all of us joining in with the staff singing happy birthday.

For a moment, I worried that Delilah might've been truly bothered by being put on the spot like that but when she took her hands away and I saw the big smile that she'd been hiding underneath, I knew we'd made the right call.

We finished the song, the manager placing the delicious-looking cake in the center of the table and lighting the twenty-one candles on top of it.

"Now," Laura said. "Pick a wish. And make it a good one."

Delilah's blue eyes flicked over to me, the smile spreading even wider before she leaned forward and blew out the candles.

"That's vanilla coconut," Archie said with a nod. "If you don't like it, pass it on over and I'll take care of it." He winked as he finished his words.

Delilah stuck her finger into the frosting, then put it in her mouth.

"It's delicious. Thank you so much."

The staff cleared the empty dinner plates from the table and replaced them with new ones. I wasn't much of a sweets guy, but the sight of the cake was enough to get my tastebuds tingling.

Delilah placed a forkful into her mouth and wrapped her lips around the end of the fork. My cock twitched as I remembered the other things she'd done recently with those lips.

I wanted her like crazy, and it was taking all my restraint to not simply take her from the table and out into the backseat of my car.

"So freaking good," Delilah said, shaking her head. "Thank you so much, Archie."

"Hey, it's my pleasure," he replied. He reached into the inner pocket of his jacket and slipped out an envelope, the words "Happy Birthday, Delilah" written on it in his neat, block handwriting. "And it's not a birthday without presents. Here."

Laura's eyes flashed. "Oh my God! How could I almost forget about presents?"

"You guys." Delilah tilted her head forward. "Seriously – I said you didn't need to worry about presents this year."

Her sisters regarded one another with a skeptical glance. "And you thought we were going to listen to you?" Maryann asked.

"Seriously," Corrine chimed in. "It's your *twenty-first* birthday. Of course we're going to get you something."

"And I didn't get that memo about not buying gifts," Archie said. "Go on and open."

A heartfelt look came over Delilah. "You guys," she said again warmly, "I don't even know what to say." She discreetly wiped a tear away, shaking her head as if unable to believe the love surrounding her in that moment.

"Alright, I won't be ungrateful. And I'm not about to start blubbering here at the table." She went to work on Archie's envelope, slitting the top open and pulling out the contents. Inside was something that resembled a credit card.

"That's a membership pass to *The Aquarium of the Pacific*," Archie said. "Good for three years. Jacob mentioned that you were into marine biology, and I figured that'd be a grand way to see it up close and personal."

Delilah's eyes lit up as she looked it over. "This is *perfect*! Thank you so much, Archie!"

He raised his glass. "Cheers."

Delilah wasn't about to let him off that easily. She got up and rushed over, throwing her arms around him, giving him a big, tight hug.

"Alright now," he said. "That'll do." The smile on his face told a different story.

"That was so sweet of you, Archie," Laura said.

"I do what I can."

The two of them shared a lingering look, and it didn't take a genius to see that there was something happening between the two of them.

"Me next!" Corrine shouted. "Now, I'm kind of a broke college student right now, so you're going to have to bear with me..."

Corrine hurried over and handed a gift bag packed with colorful paper over to her sister. Inside was a framed photograph of the three of them, perfect for her new home.

Maryann was next, her gift a spa day for the three of them next week. Delilah was thrilled.

When they were done, it was my turn. I had a gift alright, but there was only part of it I could share with her right then.

Delilah turned her eyes to me, shaking her head.

"You've done enough for me," she said. "And knowing we're going to be having a baby together is the only present I need."

"As if I'd let your twenty-first come and go without getting you a little something."

Like Archie, my gift was tucked into my suit's inner jacket pocket. I handed it over, and she took it with a curious expression on her face.

We all watched as she opened the envelope and pulled out a card. Her eyes moved over the words inside, Delilah quickly wiping away the tears at what I'd written.

"Thank you," she said. "That means a lot to me."

"I'm glad to hear it. But don't forget about the actual present."

"Oh, I won't."

The present itself was nothing special to look at – just a couple pieces of paper. But her eyes lit up when she realized what they were.

"Tickets to London?"

"That's right. We're going in two weeks, so that should give you plenty of time to get your school and work arrangements taken care of. We'll be staying in London and doing a little bit of exploring from there."

She closed her eyes, a tear trickling down her cheek.

"I don't know what to say. Thank you so much."

Delilah came over and hugged me tight, the two of us sharing a kiss while the rest of the table sounded out an "aww."

I kept the other part of the gift to myself, how I'd spoken with Helen and that she was planning on meeting with us when we came into town, but I wasn't sure quite how to broach that topic just yet.

"Alright, alright," I said, suppressing a small smile. "Show's over."

The rest of the dinner was wonderful. We ate our cake then headed back to the house for a little more celebrating.

The house was more than big enough for the whole gang to stay over and for everyone to have their own room, so I was glad to accommodate.

I abstained from drinking that night, not wanting Delilah to feel left out. Archie and Laura and the sisters got good and tipsy as they swam and soaked in the hot tub.

It wasn't long before they retired and left Delilah and me on our own, the two of us sitting on the edge of the pool with our legs dangling in the water.

My arm was wrapped around her, her head on my shoulder as we watched the outdoor lights shimmer on the surface.

"You know," she said, breaking the silence. "I think I saw Laura sneak off to Archie's room."

I chuckled. "Nothing wrong with keeping the celebration going after everyone else has gone to bed."

Delilah smiled. Then her face turned serious. She scrunched her brow, as if not knowing quite what to say next.

"Listen...this was an amazing night. One of the best birthdays I've ever had. Hell, maybe *the* best birthday. I have to admit, at first, I was a little scared of what's about to happen in my future - in *our* future. But being out with people who care about me, knowing I'm not in this alone...it goes a long way."

I leaned over and gave her a kiss on the lips.

"You're not alone. Don't ever think that."

"I won't."

She kissed me right back, the kiss quickly turning into something deeper, something more intense.

Her mouth opened and so did mine, our tongues meeting and our hands going below our waists. I couldn't help but move my fingers underneath the hem of her dress and up to the pink lingerie I knew she had on underneath.

Delilah sighed as I touched her through the fine fabric of her panties, her hair draping over my shoulder. It didn't take much touching and teasing before she came, her body tensing and releasing as the orgasm arrived.

When it was done, she spoke into my ear. "If we didn't have guests, I'd be down for doing it right here."

I grinned. "We'll have plenty of opportunities for that. Come on."

I stood and took her by the hand, bringing her to her feet and leading her back into the house. We hurried up the stairs to my bedroom, and as soon as the door was shut behind us, we couldn't take each other's clothes off fast enough.

I only had a moment to appreciate how damn good she looked in the lingerie I'd bought.

The sight of her slender, shapely body clad in it filled me with such desire that I couldn't help but rip it off.

Delilah gasped with surprise as I effortlessly pulled the lingerie off, her blue eyes wide in the low light of the room.

With a quick bend, I scooped her off her feet and carried her over to the bed. It was only a few moments until I was inside of her, Delilah's warmth wrapped around my length, her back arching as I moved inside of her, bringing her to one orgasm after another.

When I could take no more, I finished inside of her, Delilah's legs wrapping around me as she wordlessly yearned for me to stay right where I was.

We held each other for a long while afterward, her head on my chest and my hand on her back.

"Happy birthday."

She turned to me; love written all over her face.

"Thanks."

A strange tension filled the air after she spoke. I knew what to say next; I knew what was on my mind and in my heart.

I love you.

I didn't say it out loud. It was hard to tell why not.

Together, we drifted off to sleep.

"You don't have to do this," I said. It was the next morning, the two of us in the kitchen cleaning up after breakfast had been served and the guests were gone. "You've got one day left until you can march right into that bank and do whatever you want with your money. After sleeping on it, I think you should skip this last Sunday dinner and stay home. Don't give your mom the satisfaction of dancing to her tune."

Delilah hit the "start" button on the dishwasher, the machine whooshing to life.

"I see what you're saying. And yeah, you've got a point. If it were just me that she was messing with, I might agree with you. But it's not just me – it's Lila. If I don't show up, Mom's going to take that as me saying I'm fine with not seeing my little sister again. I can't do that."

I didn't necessarily agree, but I could see where she was coming from. I stepped over to her, wrapping my arms around her waist.

"You really can be too stubborn for your own good sometimes, you know?" I smiled.

She smiled back at me. "That's something you're going to have to get used to, handsome."

I leaned down and kissed her sweetly.

"OK." I took my lips from hers. "We'll go to dinner tonight. But I need to stop by the club and go over some paperwork with Archie beforehand. You OK hanging around here?"

"Sure. I was planning on grabbing lunch with Laura, and I'll come right back home after that."

"No work?" I asked.

"Told Megan that I'd need a couple of weeks off with the news about the pregnancy. Truth be told, I'm not sure I've got it in my schedule to go back."

"Think about it. I'll support you either way."

She smiled. "I know you will."

We kissed one more time before I grabbed the keys to my Bugatti and headed out. The day was perfect, the sky a clear blue, a gentle breeze coming off the ocean.

As much as I wanted to enjoy thinking about the week ahead and the trip I planned for Delilah, I knew it wasn't going to be that simple. There was still her mother to deal with, and there was no doubt in my mind that she was going to pull out all the stops in getting what she wanted.

I parked on the street across from the club, part of me wanting to take a long walk to enjoy the gorgeous day. There was too much work to be done for that, I knew. Maybe later when Archie and I had finished up.

Before I could take one step across the street, however, I heard a familiar voice call out to me.

"Jacob?"

My stomach tensed at the voice.

I turned to see Naomi making her way toward me down the sidewalk. She was dressed in expensive leisurewear, her eyes hidden behind big, designer sunglasses. If she was a woman who needed money, she sure as hell didn't look the part.

"What do you want?"

She scrunched her brow as she came to a stop in front of me, as if I'd hurt her feelings.

"Aw, are you really going to talk to me like that? I thought we were friends."

"Whatever it is, Naomi, get right to it. I've got a busy day ahead."

"That's right – and dinner after. You *are* planning on coming, aren't you?"

"We'll be there."

"Excellent. Now, I know you're a busy man. So, I will get right to it. I need the money that Delilah is coming into tomorrow. I need it desperately. Sam and I are running very low on funds, and his expansions are taking a lot longer to turn a profit than we had hoped. As it stands, we're due to run out of money before the month is over."

"Easy solution – sell the house and live within your means until you're back in the black."

She scoffed. "You don't understand, Jacob. We have images to maintain. Do you know what it would look like to our peers if we were to downgrade our lives in such a way? Unthinkable."

"I've got news for you, Naomi. If someone doesn't want to be your friend because you've fallen on some hard times, then that person was never your friend in the first place."

She snorted. "Save the Sesame Street bullshit for someone else. All it would take for this situation to go away would be for Delilah to support her own damn family."

I wasn't about to get into it with her.

"Delilah has made her feelings on the matter clear. It's up to you to accept them. We've got a child on the way to think about."

Even behind the sunglasses I could tell that she was narrowing her eyes in anger.

"You two are making a huge mistake. And don't be surprised if there's a price to pay."

With that she turned and stormed off, the red bottoms of her Louboutin's flashing behind her.

I'd told Delilah that we had one more day until we were in the clear. After my run-in with Naomi, however, I was starting to believe that we weren't even close to being in the clear as far as the matter of her mother was concerned.

CHAPTER 31

DELILAH

"Last chance, baby."

Jacob stood at the huge front doors of the mansion, looking good as ever dressed in a pair of dark slacks and an office-white dress shirt, the sleeves rolled up to the tops of his forearms in that way that never failed to make my mouth water.

Despite what was going on, my pussy clenched at the sight of him.

"I know," I said.

"We don't have to do this. You can text your mom and say you're not coming. Nothing's stopping you."

He was right – it would be as simple as a single text message, but I couldn't do it.

"It's Lila."

He nodded, then stepped over to me and placed his hands on my shoulders.

"I understand."

Anger ran through me, making my skin hot.

"I hate this. I hate that she's so willing to use my little sister, her

206 | K.C. CROWNE

own daughter, to get what she wants. Who the hell does something like that? Doesn't it occur to her how evil it is?"

He formed his mouth into a hard line for a long moment, and I could sense that he was just as angry about it as I was. No doubt he was choosing his words carefully.

"Some people will do whatever it takes to get what they want, and that includes using others as tools then tossing them aside when they're done. It sounds to me like your mother is focused on the money, and whatever collateral damage she causes in the process is justified in her mind. But maybe she'll come around. Maybe tonight, you'll be able to talk some sense into her."

I shook my head. "Not a chance. Mom's been like this since I've been old enough to remember. No way in hell she'd ever change her ways."

"Then we're just going to have to deal with it. We'll go, and when you're ready to leave, we will. All you have to do is say the word."

"Thanks. This isn't going to be easy. And I'm sure she's going to use every little trick she has up her sleeve to get me to crack. But I won't let her."

"That's right. And don't forget that you're not going through this alone."

He squeezed my shoulders one more time, leaning in and giving me a gentle kiss.

"You've got this."

With that, we left the house.

The sun was setting over the water as we drove, the deep, blood red at the horizon, giving way to a creamy orange and endless purple above. It would've been a gorgeous evening to go to the beach, to have dinner at some café on the shore – anything other than going to see my mother and getting grilled about my future.

Jacob held my hand as he drove, his touch putting me at ease. By the time we arrived at Mom's house, I felt as ready as I was going to be.

"Remember," he said. "You don't have to put up with any bullshit. Whenever you want to go, just say the word and we're out of there. It's never too late to turn a bad evening into a good one."

I leaned over and kissed him. "Let's do this."

We climbed out of the car, the evening well into darkness as we made our way to the house. The door opened as we approached, Sam greeting us.

"Hey there, you two," he said. "Come on in!"

"Good to see you, Sam," said Jacob.

"Yeah," I echoed. "Good to see you."

"We've got the BBQ going, all the gang's out back. Go ahead and grab whatever you want to drink from the kitchen." He flashed a big, toothy smile. "I got some root beers for you, Delilah, since you're not drinking booze and all."

"Thanks," I said smiling back.

Truth be told, Sam didn't seem like a bad guy, and I hated that he was wrapped up in my mother's web.

Jacob and I went through the kitchen, both of us grabbing root beers as we made our way out to the backyard.

Sure enough, the whole gang was there. Corrine and Maryann were seated on either side of Mom, who was in the center of the big, circular table with Lila on her lap.

She reminded me of a mob boss, sitting right in the middle, looking completely calm and in control.

"There you are," she said, a pleased smile on her face. "We were all wondering when you were going to get here. Have a seat – there's plenty of food to go around."

Jacob and I shared a look that suggested we both sensed something strange was up. What was going on, and why was she being so nice?

Did Mom have some new angle she was trying out? Or was she regarding us with the certainty of a hunter watching her prey march straight into a trap?

Not knowing what else to do, I made myself a plate and sat down, though eating was the last thing on my mind.

Mom started the conversation lightly, asking my sisters questions about their work and school and what they had planned for the summer ahead. Their answers were a bit guarded, and I could tell by the tone of their voices that they sensed something was up, too.

I took a bite of my hot dog, though I wasn't hungry in the slightest.

"So, Delilah." Mom using my full name like that was more than enough to put me on edge. "Are you getting excited about motherhood? And how's your morning sickness been?"

Lila gurgled and babbled on Mom's lap. Just the idea of never seeing my little sister again was enough to make me hurt inside in a way I could hardly stand.

"My morning sickness?" I asked. "It's been better, now that you mention it. And yeah, I'm excited."

Jacob spoke up. "You want to tell your mom about your birthday gift?"

Mom arched an eyebrow. "Birthday gift? That's right, it was your birthday yesterday. Sorry for not saying anything – we've been a little busy around here with the businesses and Lila. And money's a little tight for gifts."

I winced at her words, knowing it was the first volley of what I had no doubt would be a full-on assault that would take place by the end of the night. All I could do was brace myself.

"Now," she said. "What about this birthday present? I'm sure a man like Jacob was able to treat you to something very nice."

"Jacob and I are going to London for two weeks. It's going to be a lot of fun."

Mom's face flashed with anger for a brief moment, but she quickly regained her calm and composure.

"That sounds wonderful. Maybe you and your grandmother can spend some time together, discuss how much fun it is for you both not to support your family when they need it."

Lots of choice words came to mind, but I held them all back.

"I haven't spoken to Grandma, actually. Not like you'll give me her number to get in touch with her."

"It's really for the best that you don't have contact with her. You remind me of her in ways that I most definitely do not like."

I glanced over at Jacob, who said nothing. He was as cool and composed as ever.

He quickly made eye contact with me, and I could sense that he was saying, without words, "you've got this." It made me feel so much better knowing that he had my back.

Mom sighed, then took a sip of her wine.

"Listen, Delilah. Believe it or not, I want to have a nice night with you and the rest of the family. All the same, I'd be doing myself and Sam a disservice if I didn't ask one last time if you were going to be helping us with our money issues. You can say yes, or you can say no. But either way, I'll drop the matter."

I cocked my head to the side. I wasn't sure if I'd heard her correctly.

"You're going to drop it? So, if I were to say no right here and now, you'd accept that and leave me alone?"

Mom nodded. "That's right. What do you say? You want to do the right thing and help out your own mother? Your own flesh and blood?"

Silence hung in the air, along with a great deal of tension. Underneath the table, Jacob took my hand giving it a squeeze.

"No. Sorry, Mom. But I'm not going to do it. It would kill me if you told me that I couldn't see Lila, but I'm not going to let you use her as a bargaining chip to get what you want. Be mad at me if that's what you need to do, but you have my answer."

God, it felt good to lay it out for her in such a simple way. All the same, the silence that followed was enough to put me ill at ease.

Mom sat there with a small smile on her face, Lila reaching up at her. She was glaring at me in a way that said, "this isn't over."

"That's fine. It's your money, and therefore it's your decision." She shrugged.

Mom took another sip of wine, and I shared another glance with Jacob.

He spoke up next. "Well, I'm sure I can speak for Delilah when I say we're both pleased that you've come around on the matter. Trust me, as a business owner, ups and downs are all part of the process. You'll both be fine – I'm sure of it."

Sam smiled. "Very nice of you to say, Jacob. So, tell me more about this trip you two have planned..."

With that, dinner continued. Jacob outlined the trip, how we'd be staying in the heart of London and taking in all the sights.

Maryann and Corrine had their questions too, which Jacob happily answered. Mom was true to her word, not mentioning the money at any point throughout dinner.

In fact, she didn't say much of anything. Instead, she sipped her wine and fed Lila a bottle when she wanted it. Before too long, the dinner was over, and Jacob and I were back in the car on our way home.

We shared a look the moment we were on our way that made it clear we both had the same thought on our minds.

"That was *weird*." He was the first one to break the silence, but he'd said exactly what I was thinking.

"So weird. I was dead certain that Mom was going to come after me with all she had."

Jacob said nothing as he drove south, starting on Santa Monica back to the PCH.

"Your mom may not be done with us just yet. Tonight might've been her last shot at playing nice."

"You think she's going to try something else?"

"I'm not sure. You know her best. But I've dealt with enough scheming types to know that they never give up that easily. In fact, one of their most reliable tricks is letting you think that they've given up."

"Because that makes you let your guard down."

"Right. So, let's keep our eyes open. Until your name is on the dotted line at the bank tomorrow, we both need to be on our guard."

He was right. Jacob was good like that, always working out all the angles.

"Anyway, I had an idea."

"What's that?"

He smiled. "I've got a meeting up in Seattle this weekend. If you're not too busy with school, I was thinking you could come with."

"Wow – a vacation before a vacation? You're spoiling me, Mr. Nichols."

"Let me ask you this, when was the last time you've been on a vacation?"

I had to really think about it. "God, it had to be back in my sophomore year. Mom took all of us to San Jose so she could meet this guy she'd been talking to online. It wasn't much of a trip, really. We just bummed around at this guy's house while he and Mom ran around town."

"Let me get this straight – the last vacation you had was your mom dragging you along on a booty call?"

I couldn't help but laugh. "Yep, more or less."

He shook his head, the smirk still on his face.

"And here you are, telling me I'm spoiling you. From where I sit, you're due for a hell of a lot of spoiling to make up for lost time."

CHAPTER 32

JACOB

Music was playing, food was cooking, and the sun was coming up in the east, filling the kitchen with brilliant, golden light. It was already shaping up to be a perfect day, and I was planning on keeping it that way.

Classic jazz played from the Sonos as I flipped pancakes on the griddle, the smell of fresh coffee in the air. I couldn't help but smile as I got it all ready.

"Pancakes? Really?" I turned to see Delilah at the entrance to the kitchen. She was dressed in nothing but one of my T-shirts, the hem cutting off just below where her panties would've been.

The sight was almost enough to make me flip one of the pancakes straight into the ceiling.

"Really." I gestured toward the coffee machine, letting her know it was ready to pour. "This is a special day, and we're going to treat it like one."

An interested expression took hold. "Tell me more, Mr. Nichols."

"First, we're doing breakfast here – pancakes, as you can see. Then we're heading to the bank and getting all the paperwork handled. Once that's done, we're meeting with my personal accountant in West Hollywood. There, we'll get your money set up so that it's not just sitting around – it'll be making a profit for you. After that, we're going to stop for lunch on Rodeo drive, followed by a walk up to the Griffith Observatory. Then dinner in Newport. Sound good?"

Her eyes widened. "That sounds perfect."

"Great. All you have to do is eat and get dressed. I'll handle the rest."

She smiled, sitting down at the kitchen bar with a cup of coffee as I set a plate in front of her.

"Thanks, Jacob. Really."

I leaned over the counter and planted a kiss on her lips.

"My pleasure. Last thing I want is you stressing out on a day like today."

I finished preparing the food and we ate, Delilah taking over the stereo and putting on some 90's R&B. The music wasn't my taste, but her happiness was infectious.

When we were finished eating, I cleaned up as she showered and threw on some clothes. A little before nine, we were off.

We headed to the West Hollywood branch of her bank, arriving a little before nine-thirty. I could tell she was tense, and I made sure to take her hand as we stepped into the small, well-lit office with the bank representative.

Over the course of the next twenty minutes or so, the representative walked Delilah through the will, informing her about what her grandparents had left to her. The amount was impressive – mid six-figures and more than enough to cover her college expenses.

Seeing the amount in front of her was enough to make Delilah go wide-eyed, and I made sure to sweep in and ask some questions that she might need to know the answers to.

A few signatures later and the money was hers, wired right into her bank account and ready to spend. We had a little time before we were set to meet with my accountant, so we stopped for coffee after finishing up at the bank.

Delilah sipped her decaf, staring off into space. No doubt she'd need time to process what had just happened.

"So," I said, breaking the silence. "Got any ideas what you want to do first with the money?"

She pursed her lips and glanced away, thinking it over.

"School," she said with a confident nod. "That's the first thing. I want to get a Ph.D., so that's where some of the money is going. After that...I don't know. What the hell does anyone even do with that kind of money?"

"Hey, you're in LA – you could blow it in a night if you wanted."

She laughed. "Not that kind of girl."

"Well, when we meet with my accountant, he'll have all kinds of suggestions. The key is to beat inflation – get some good investments lined up. You play your cards right and you can double what you have in a few years."

That got her attention. "*Double?* Are you serious?"

"It'd take some work, but yeah. Cherry Lane makes good money, but it's only a small percentage of my income. The rest comes from stocks, property investments, equity in companies. You're smart with that cash and you'll have enough to live on for the rest of your life. Assuming your tastes don't get too expensive, that is."

She said nothing, giving one slow, hard blink, her mouth in a flat line.

"OK, now I'm really glad you're here to walk me through this. The most money I've ever had is like, two-thousand dollars. And even that seemed like a lot."

I put my hand on her leg and gave it a squeeze. "It'll be fine. The biggest mistake I've seen people make with money they've come into is not getting an accountant and making smart choices of what to do with it. Believe me, in my business there's no shortage of young men who come into a few million through lucky investments or crypto and end up throwing it all away at clubs like mine."

She grinned. "Alright, so step one is don't spend a bunch of money at strip clubs."

That got a laugh out of me. "Right. But hey, if you want to stop by Cherry Lane, I'll make sure to give you a little discount."

Delilah grinned even bigger, giving me a playful punch in the arm.

"OK," she said. "I'm ready to do this."

With that, we left the coffee shop and headed toward the office of my accountant, Jared Mayer.

He welcomed us inside, and we wasted no time getting to down to business.

"That was a lot," Delilah said, after we had finished with Jared. We were seated near one of the big front windows of a restaurant on Rodeo Drive. "Jared was awesome explaining everything, but even so I feel like my head's spinning."

"That's understandable. You're entering a new world now," I said. "Having money is great but learning how to be responsible with it can feel overwhelming."

She took my hand and squeezed. "Thanks for helping me out with all of this."

I squeezed her hand right back. "It's my pleasure – really. I've got no doubt you're going to handle the learning curve. And you're going to end up having more money than you know what to do with. Parlay one property investment into a few others and ten years from now you could be looking at a seven-figure net worth."

Her eyes flashed. "That's insane. I don't even know what I'd do with that much money."

"Don't worry about it right now. You'll have more than enough time to wrap your head arou-"

"No, wait, I know what I want to do with it." There was total determination in her voice, and not a shred of doubt.

"What's that?"

"I want to make a difference."

Her voice was filled with so much certainty, so much passion, that I couldn't help but want to hear more.

"Tell me."

"I was actually lucky. My sisters and I came from a hard place with no dad and a mom who was more concerned about her next shopping spree sugar daddy than providing for our future. But I was fortunate enough to have grandparents who looked out for me, who set aside money for us to build a future."

I said nothing, listening intently.

"But for every woman like me who was lucky enough to have that kind of support, I know there has to be tons of others who aren't as fortunate. I want to start something, some kind of foundation, where I can support those girls."

"Like a scholarship fund."

Her eyes lit up with excitement, her blues brilliant in the afternoon light. I loved seeing the eagerness on her gorgeous face.

"That's it! I want to start a scholarship fund where girls who've come from difficult backgrounds can have financial support to pursue their dreams."

I loved the idea and her passion for it.

"That's going to be a lot of work. You're going to need not only money, but some experience in setting up a foundation. Not to mention finding good people to help you run it."

"Fine. I'm not worried about a little hard work."

"I've no doubt about that. And I'm going to support you the whole way. But take it one step at a time; don't rush into anything."

"Right. I still need to finish school and get my Ph.D. Then I've got to wait for all these investments to flourish. One thing at a time, right?"

"Now you're thinking like an investor."

Delilah wasn't the first person I'd met with over the years to coach them on investing. But she was, far and away, the one with the best head on her shoulders. I didn't have a single doubt that she'd kick ass.

I was also thrilled at the idea of being at her side while she did it.

We finished up our lunch, Delilah talking my ear off in the best way possible about all the good things she wanted to do with her money. I listened to every word, loving what I was hearing.

After lunch, it was time for our walk. I was eager to get out for some fresh air after being cooped up in stuffy offices all day.

"Mind if I drive?" she asked as we approached my car. "I'm kind of feeling like being in the driver's seat."

I raised an eyebrow, intrigued by her suggestion. "You serious?"

Delilah winked. "Does it look like I'm joking?"

"Not at all. Just that this is a lot of car to handle."

"Sounds like a challenge."

"You ever driven a stick before?"

"Learned to drive on my mom's old Impala. I can shift with the best of 'em."

I tossed my keys over, and she neatly caught them. "Let's see what you've got."

With that, we climbed into the car. It was strange being in the passenger seat of the Bugatti – I'd always been the driver of my vehicles.

I watched as Delilah turned over the engine, a wicked smile forming on her lips as she started it up and put the car into gear.

She pulled out of the parking spot, guiding it toward the road. Moments later we were out on Fairfax, the engine revving as she drove north. Delilah drove like a pro, the smile staying on her face as she carefully moved from one lane to the other, the engine growling as she shifted.

"This is awesome!" she shouted. "Maybe I'll trade in the BMW for one of these!"

I laughed. As I watched her, the feeling of total love gripped my heart. I'd known, deep down, for quite some time that I loved her. Yet for whatever reason I hadn't told her.

Was I scared? Was putting my heart out on the line too much for me to take?

It didn't matter, I decided. I loved this woman and every day that went by without her knowing was a crime. I'd tell her that night.

I'd look into her eyes and let her know she was the woman I wanted to spend the rest of my life with, and that I was thrilled to be the father of her child.

I glanced over at her, drinking in her beauty. As Delilah pulled the car onto Hollywood Boulevard, a small, black sedan zipped through the red light, barreling toward us.

It didn't stop.

"Delilah!"

Her name was the last thing that came out of my mouth before the car smashed into ours. The breaking of glass and the grinding of metal-on-metal filled the air, only blackness following.

CHAPTER 33

DELILAH

My body ached everywhere – that was the first thing I noticed.

The second, when I opened my eyes, was that I was in a hospital room.

I let out a groan, trying to remember what had happened.

I gingerly turned my head to see Jacob seated in the corner of the room, leaning forward with his hands clasped between his legs. His eyes were on me, watching me carefully.

"Easy," he said, his voice low and calm and reassuring. "Easy."

The situation began to dawn on me through my muddled mind, panic soon following.

"Where am I?" I asked. As soon as the words were out of my mouth, I understood how silly they were. I took more of my surroundings in. My head pounded, and I noticed that my left forearm was in a cast. I tried to turn, but my neck was stuck in some kind of brace. "What time is it?"

"You're in Memorial Regional Hospital," he said. "And it's almost sunset." He looked me over, his eyes filled with concern. I could sense that, whatever emotions were running through him, he was doing his best to keep them in check.

I was so worried I could hardly think straight, especially through the pain.

"One second," he said, holding up a finger as he hurried over to the door and opened it. "Hey! She's up!"

Before I knew what was happening, a pair of nurses rushed into the room and began looking me over.

That's when it occurred to me.

The baby.

A fear like I'd never known before in my life took hold, my stomach tightening and my blood running cold.

"My baby?" I asked. "What happened to my baby?" I was so scared that part of me wished I hadn't even asked the question.

"You're fine," said one of the nurses. "The baby's fine."

All the energy drained out of my body as if someone had pulled a plug. My arms and legs went limp, and tears formed in my eyes. One of the nurses noticed, pulling a handful of tissues from a nearby box and placing them in my hand. I wasted no time wiping the tears away.

"You know for sure?"

"Yeah," Jacob said as he opened his hand to take the tissues. "They checked when you got here. We were lucky - the accident could've been much worse."

"We've been keeping a very close eye on the baby," said one of the nurses. "And he's right – it's pure luck that the both of you are OK."

"But the baby's totally fine? Nothing's wrong?" It occurred to me then that I hadn't asked about my own injuries.

I realized, however, that I didn't give a damn about those. All I cared about was the little boy or girl inside of me.

"Nothing at all," said the other nurse. "The brunt of the collision hit the back driver's side door, and not you."

"The baby's fine," the first nurse reiterated. "You, my dear, are a different story."

Knowing my baby was alright made me ready for any news.

"What happened?"

"Broken forearm, minor concussion, and a fractured collarbone," she said. "And some major bruising."

"Tell me," the other nurse said. "What do you remember?"

I closed my eyes, trying to piece together what had happened that resulted in my being in the hospital. Everything was strange and muddy.

I looked over at Jacob. "There was the meeting with the accountant; I remember that. Then we had lunch...I drove your car...and that's it."

"Someone barreled through the intersection at Fairfax and Hollywood," Jacob filled in the blanks. "Smashed right into us."

"What?" I couldn't believe what I was hearing. I tried to remember, but nothing came to mind. It frustrated me like crazy that I couldn't piece together what had happened. I felt helpless. "Who did it? Some drunk driver?"

Jacob didn't answer at first, instead clenching his jaw and working through the anger that was obviously taking hold.

"We don't know. I was conscious through it all, and whoever hit us drove out of there as fast as they could. I managed to get a shot of the car, sent it to a contact I have in the LAPD. We'll know soon enough."

"You're not thinking it was on purpose?" I asked.

"Don't know. But I'm not going to rest until I find the prick who put you and our child in danger."

His hands were balled into fists, and I had no doubt that he meant his words. Jacob stepped over to the window, the view looking out over Hollywood, and took a moment to compose himself.

"We're going to keep you for a few days to monitor your concussion and the baby," one of the nurses said.

Hearing that, I felt much more at ease.

"Just relax and get comfortable. And you might not feel like it right now, but it's a good idea to try to get some solid food in you before too long."

"Yeah. I'll work my way up to it."

The nurses left, letting me know that they were nearby if I needed anything, and that they'd be back in a little bit to run some tests.

Jacob still stood by the window, his back to me. Silence filled the room.

"Jacob," I said. "Are you OK?"

His big shoulders rose and fell as he took in a deep breath. Then he looked back at me.

"I'm fine. But you almost weren't. I should've been the one behind the wheel. I shouldn't have let you drive." There was anger in his voice, and I could sense it was all directed at himself.

"It wasn't your fault. There's no way you could've known that something like that was going to happen. Some jerk blew through the intersection, probably drunk. And think about it – if you would've told me that you weren't going to let me drive, do you think I would've listened?" I followed this up with a smile, and he gave me a small one of his own. "Come over here."

Jacob turned from the window and stepped over to me. I noticed for the first time that his shirt had been ripped, that a small bit of dried blood was on the sleeve.

"What happened?" I asked.

"Huh?" he glanced down at where I'd been looking. "Oh. It's nothing. Scratched myself on the metal while I was pulling you out of the car."

"You pulled me out? God, you're like a superhero or something."

He shrugged again, and I couldn't help but find his humbleness charming.

"You're all that matters," he said. "You and the baby." He sat down on the edge of the bed, the mattress sagging slightly under his solidity. "When I'd looked over and saw you in the driver's seat lying still, I..." he trailed off, as if he didn't even want to finish.

I took his hand. "That didn't happen. I'm fine; the baby's fine."

He glanced down and nodded, and I could sense that he was still having a hard time with how close he'd come to losing me. It moved me to see how deeply he cared.

Jacob cleared his throat and spoke.

"Before the accident, I told myself that I was going to say something to you later today when the time was right. And over the last few hours here, not knowing for sure when you were going to wake up, all I could think about was how I hadn't told you what I'd wanted to because I didn't know how to handle what I was feeling for you."

I didn't know what to say. So, I said nothing, letting him go on.

He turned to me, warmth in his eyes.

"I love you, Delilah. I love you like I've never loved anyone in my life. This engagement might've been a sham, but there's no doubt in my mind that I want to spend the rest of my life with you – if you'll have me."

I smiled, tears welling in my eyes.

"There's nothing I want more, either. And I love you, too."

He leaned in and kissed me gently. Despite it all, the moment was perfect.

CHAPTER 34

JACOB

One week later...

"I'm so sorry. I wish I would've known, Jacob. You have to believe me."

Two emotions were present in the air as I sat with Sam in the office of my club – his fear, and my rage.

I wasn't angry at him. No, he was the one who was giving me the proper outlet for my anger.

"You're telling me Naomi did all of this behind your back?"

He nodded, fear in his eyes.

"We talked about her and Delilah; I thought she'd finally accepted that Delilah wasn't going to give her any money. I'd sat down with her last Sunday morning, talked to her about what we'd do if Delilah told her no one last time." He shook his head. "I said that we'd have to sell the house, make some lifestyle adjustments. And she'd seemed totally fine with it. That should've been my warning."

I took a deep, slow breath. Rage boiled inside of me, but I didn't want to take it out on Sam.

"All the while," I said, "she was working behind your back planning to pay some asshole to try and kill her own daughter."

It was almost too much to take. Never in a million years would I have thought a woman could treat her own flesh and blood that way, putting her daughter's life and the life of her grandchild at risk.

"How did you find out?"

He let out a snort, shaking his head. "Happenstance. I was doing a check on one of the stores, the one in Newport, and I saw Naomi's car there. Now, she's never showed a damn bit of interest in doing any work with my shops – they were money sources, and that was all. So, I followed her car and watched her pull into a back alley where she met with him." He pointed to the folder on my desk.

I opened the folder again, looking down at the face of the man who'd nearly killed the woman I loved. Just laying eyes on the picture was enough to fill me with a rage unlike anything I'd ever experienced.

"And you're positive that's what they were planning?"

"Almost certain. I can't see any other reason why she'd be meeting with one of my warehouse guys. Just to be on the safe side, I pulled him aside once he was back at the job site, asked him where he was Sunday night, that sort of thing. He was cagey, got really nervous."

I closed the folder and pushed it aside.

"I'll figure out one way or another," I said. "I can be very persuasive when it comes to getting information. Now, tell me why you think she did this."

He shook his head. "I don't know. And really, I don't even want to think about it. Maybe she just wanted to scare her; maybe she viewed the baby as a threat, blocking her from getting at the money. Maybe she wanted to try and kill you."

"Lots of motives," I agreed. "I'll get to the bottom of it."

Sam shook his head in disbelief. "I can't believe I've gotten involved with a woman like this. And my daughter..."

My focus was on bringing Naomi and the driver to justice for what they'd done, but there was still the matter of Sam and Lila.

"Can you run your business from outside of the city?"

"Sure, I suppose."

"Then you're going to Seattle for the month. Get what you need from your house, and I'll send you the flight and accommodation information. I'm going to handle this, and I'll give you the all clear to come back to LA when it's done."

"Lila," he said. "What about her?"

"She'll stay with Delilah and me until we can get Naomi taken care of and you settled. It's the best way to keep her safe. Naomi's already shown what she's capable of, and I'm not taking any chances."

The relief on his face was palpable. "Thank you."

"We'll help you figure out Lila's future later. But when this is all said and done, I'll make sure that your financial situation's covered, so you don't need to worry about where your daughter's next meal is coming from."

"God, thank you so much."

We shook, and that was the end of the meeting. I called for Archie as Sam left.

"What's the word, boss?"

I rose, folder in hand. "I want you to track this man down. Find some place good and private to take him for questioning. But before that, get Sam on the next flight to Seattle, find someplace safe for him to stay. And arrange for Lila to be taken to the Malibu house."

"Got it, boss."

He left, and I was alone. I gave myself a moment to let the anger work through my system.

I had planned on going back to the hospital after speaking with Sam and didn't want to bring any negative energy there with me. When I was ready, I sent a text to Delilah letting her know that my meeting was over.

I'd tell her the nature of my meeting in time. For now, I wanted to make sure my suspicion was confirmed.

I drove my new car - a dark green Jaguar convertible - from the club back to the hospital. I felt better the moment I saw the building, knowing that my love was inside.

On the way in, one of the nurses who'd been looking after her stopped me to let me know that Delilah had been given the all clear to check out that evening.

It was the best news I could imagine. She was on the mend, the baby still good and healthy.

I was ready to get her home.

Loud noises of surprise and happiness exploded from down the hall. I listened carefully, hearing the familiar voices of Maryann and Corrine. That wasn't a surprise – they'd been there when I'd left a couple of hours ago.

There was another voice as well, one that I couldn't quite pinpoint but that sounded familiar all the same.

I made my way to the room and stepped inside.

"And there's the man himself."

There was a guest in the room – Delilah's grandmother, Helen. She turned with a smile on her face, her eyes the same brilliant blue as her granddaughter's.

"Helen," I said, stepping over and offering my hand. "It's a pleasure to finally meet you in person."

She glanced down at my hand, narrowing her eyes with a smile on her face.

"Put that mitt away, Jacob, and give me a hug."

I did as I was told, opening my arms, and embracing her.

"Did you know she was coming?" Delilah asked, her bed pushed up into a sitting position.

"I did," I said. "We had big plans for us to meet during our London trip. But things changed."

"Right," Helen said. "And some road raging prick almost took my granddaughter from me." She sighed, shaking her head.

Corrine's eyes lit up. "OK! So, what's the plan?"

"Yeah!" Maryann jumped in. The sisters were different in their own ways, but I loved how they shared the same energy and enthusiasm. "They said that Des was finally getting out today."

"That's what I just heard, too," I replied. "I don't know about you all, but I could sure go for a quiet night in and some food that wasn't made in a hospital kitchen." The sisters made various noises of agreement. "And Helen, I sincerely hope that you didn't get a hotel room while you're in town."

"You kidding?" she asked with a smile. "Delilah tells me you've got a beachfront mansion in Malibu. Not a chance I'm staying at a Holiday Inn now."

"Then it's settled. And ladies, you're all more than welcome to stay for as long as you want."

"You're going to have to kick us out," Maryann added with a smile.

"And we're going to have another guest," I said. "Lila's going to be joining us later today."

That got some confused looks.

"Lila?" Delilah asked.

"We'll talk about it later tonight. But Sam's going out of town and asked me if we'd be fine taking her for a bit."

I'd have to tell them the whole situation later once we were settled at home.

"Sounds great!" Delilah said. "Now, can we get the heck out of here?"

With that, we started the discharge process of checking Delilah out. The doctors came to give her and the baby one more checkup – the baby was fine, and Delilah was healing nicely.

Once that was done, we finished up the paperwork and headed out. The convoy of our three cars headed to Malibu, relief washing over me as I laid eyes on the place.

"God, it feels good to be back," Delilah said as we stepped out of the car.

Helen put her hands on her hips and looked the house over. "Damn! You weren't kidding when you said he had a Malibu mansion."

I chuckled. "Ladies, let me handle the bags."

Once we were inside, I gave Helen the grand tour and let her have her pick of the rooms. When we were alone, she approached me in a conspiratorial manner.

"Got a little something for you," she said, opening the back zipper of her bag and pulling out a small, black box.

I couldn't help but grin at the sight of it.

"Helen, I could kiss you."

She held up her hand. "Save it for the mother-to-be, lover boy."

I laughed as I stepped over to her. She placed the box in my hand, and I wasted no time opening it and taking a look inside.

It was perfect.

The evening was wonderful - relaxing and mellow.

We ordered some pizza from a local place, the ladies, aside from Delilah, having some wine while they all caught up with one another.

As they relaxed poolside, Archie arrived with Laura - the two of them now an item, it would seem - with baby gear in tow to get set up for Lila's arrival later that night.

Lila showed up at around eight, Sam dropping her off before taking his flight to Seattle. He was shaken but relieved to know his daughter would be in good hands.

Naomi was in Vegas for the weekend, so she wouldn't know a thing.

Everyone ended up staying over, and when they'd all gone to bed, it was just Delilah and me. The gift from Helen was burning a hole in my pocket, and by the time we were alone, I could hardly wait to share it with her.

"Hey, mind coming out back with me?"

230 | K.C. CROWNE

Delilah glanced up from the sink where she was in the middle of scrubbing dishes and putting them into the washer.

"Uh, sure."

We stepped out back, the evening perfect. The air was cool, the moon full and high above.

"What's up?" she asked.

Delilah placed her hand on her belly in the way that she'd been doing over the last couple of weeks, as if providing an extra layer of protection and care for our child. I loved it.

"I've never been good at things like this."

"Like what?" she reached over and took my hand, squeezing it tightly.

"Like telling people how I feel about them."

She smiled softly, warmly. "Just let go and say what comes to mind."

"I love you. That's what comes to mind."

Her smile brightened, tears forming in her eyes. "And I love you."

The words made me feel a way I didn't know it was possible to feel. I had to go on – telling her I loved her wasn't all I had on my mind.

The anxiety had melted away. Only eagerness and excitement remained.

I couldn't wait to show her what I had.

"I love you," I said again. "I can't wait to start our family. And if you'll have me, I want you to be my wife."

I took the small, black box out of my pocket, opening it and revealing the ring inside. It was Helen's ring, the one she'd planned to pass down to Delilah, with whom she'd had a special bond.

Just as I'd hoped, Delilah's eyes lit up. Tears formed again, her hands shooting to her mouth.

"That's Grandma Helen's ring! How did you..."

"Don't worry about how. Just think about what you want."

She turned her eyes from the ring to me. "Of course I want to marry you, duh!"

I laughed. Delilah threw her arms around me, and we kissed madly, my hands somehow managing to work the ring onto her finger. Only joy lay ahead. I could feel it.

EPILOGUE I

DELILAH

Six weeks later...

"I promise I'll be gentle."

I groaned, frustrated. "I'm tired of gentle."

Jacob chuckled. "I know, princess, but you're still healing. There will be plenty of time to be not so gentle later."

I loved the way he looked at me, like I was the only woman in the world. It didn't hurt that I could feel his hardness pressing against my thigh either.

I was turned on like mad, and though I was eager to get to the doctor and have this damned cast cut off, I wanted something else first.

"We can wait," he said. "We've got the whole day ahead of us."

I pursed my lips, my hand moving under the covers and taking hold of him. His luscious lips formed into a smile, and I could tell that he was just as excited as I was.

My womanhood was already wet, but touching his cock made me practically soaked.

"So," I said, stroking him slowly. "What's the plan for today?"

He chuckled. "You really want to do this now?"

"Of course, I do. You know I'm nothing if not organized."

He formed his lips into a flat line and closed his eyes for a moment, letting out a low growl as I stroked him. Then, as if coming to his senses, he opened his eyes again.

"Well, there's Lila. Got to change and feed her and get her ready for the day."

"Right," I said. "And don't forget that Sam's out of town this next week, so we've got her two weeks in a row."

"Right. Then there's the doctor's office."

"Mmm-hmm. And lunch with my sisters after so they can take Lila for the afternoon."

"Then...shit. What was next?"

"How could you forget? We're meeting with that stationary artist to look at invitations. I know the wedding's not until fall, but it's going to come before you know it."

"Speaking of coming before you know it..."

I laughed.

"Seriously," he said. "You've come a long way from being a clueless virgin."

"I was *not* clueless," I said. "And you'd better be careful with what you say when I've got your cock in my hand."

"Good point."

"Then we're doing dinner with Archie and Laura. You remembered that, right?"

"Sure did." He closed his eyes once more, focusing on my touch. "Now that we've got our schedule sorted out, let's move on to more pressing matters."

"Gladly."

He reached down and took my hand from his cock. I was confused at first, but when he began to move down, I understood just what my handsome fiancé had in mind.

He pushed the sheets aside, and I glanced down to watch as he spread my legs open and positioned himself between my thighs.

My belly had gotten bigger, and I knew it was only a matter of time before I wouldn't be able to see him as he pleased me.

Jacob brushed my thighs with his mouth, teasing my clit with his finger before bringing his mouth to it. His tongue moved expertly over me, tracing big circles around my most intimate parts, pleasure moving through my body in warm waves.

"You know," he said, taking his lips away for a moment. "You taste even better than usual."

He flashed me a grin before going back to work, covering my lips and clit in kisses as he pushed two of his fingers inside of me.

My walls gripped him tightly as he curled his fingers and began teasing my G-spot, his tongue still working its magic. Now and then he'd take his fingers out, replacing them with his tongue, darting it in and out of me.

It was too much to bear. "Jacob," I moaned. "Please, don't stop."

My words only made him work harder, and in the middle of a hard press of his tongue against my clit, my orgasm rushed free and swept through my body.

I grabbed my breasts, squeezing them tightly as I came. The pleasure rose and fell, and his timing was so perfect that right as I wanted more, he was already on top of me.

"I can't wait any longer," I said. "I need it."

He grinned in the way he always did when the foreplay had brought me to the point where all I wanted was for his cock to be buried deep inside of me.

"Then show me."

My legs spread, I took hold of his cock and guided it right to my opening. My eyes closed, I placed his head between my lips, the put my hands on his ass. With a slow push, I guided him into me.

He felt so damn good inside of me, his thick cock stretching me open as it always did. When he was buried to the hilt, I opened my eyes to see him just above me, his gaze locked on mine.

"You're so damn beautiful," he said. "So damn perfect. I can't believe you're all mine."

His words took me to another level. In that moment, all I felt was joy.

"Right back at you, Mr. Nichols."

"I love you, baby."

"And I love you."

We kissed hard and deep as he moved in me, his cock pushing in and out, his thickness guiding me closer and closer to the perfect orgasm that I knew awaited me.

Sex between us was something special, something that I was so happy I only had shared with him.

I watched the muscles of his perfect body work, my breasts bouncing with each thrust, his manhood vanishing into me over and over and over again.

"Come for me, baby," he growled into my ear, his hot breath making me tingle all over.

I did as he asked, the eruption of ecstasy blasting through my body in hot pulses. Jacob came with me, his body tensing as his cock throbbed inside of me, his warmth coating my walls and taking my orgasm to another level.

As our breathing returned to normal, he curled up beside me, wrapping me in his big arm and pulling me close. I draped my leg over his middle, and we kissed slowly and tenderly like we were the only damn people in the world.

I turned from him, resting my head on his chest, and looking around. The room was quiet, golden beams of sunlight cutting through the air, the hush of the waves crashing into the shore sounding in the distance.

My life was perfect.

I had a fiancé that I loved like crazy, a family that cared about me, and a baby on the way. The memories from our London trip were still fresh in my mind, and we were already planning our honeymoon.

Only Lila's whimper from the nanny cam app on my phone broke the silence.

"I'll get her," he said. "You take your time."

He gave me a quick kiss on the lips before hopping out of bed. I let my eyes linger on his perfect butt as he hurried to the bathroom to grab a robe.

I considered how damn lucky I was that I'd be seeing that gorgeous behind of his every damn day for the rest of my life.

I only dawdled for a few minutes before stepping out of bed, grabbing my robe, and wrapping it on before stepping into my slippers.

The sounds of soft singing greeted me as I approached the nursery, and when I entered the room, I watched as Jacob delicately and carefully changed Lila's diaper, singing a song to her before kissing her on the forehead.

When he was done, he dressed the baby and held her close, bringing her out onto the balcony.

The sight was like none other. The way he was with Lila was a soft side that I knew he didn't show to anyone.

It made me damn certain he'd be the best dad ever.

I stepped out onto the balcony, Lila reaching out to me and cooing. I kissed her, then kissed my love.

Life was wonderful.

EPILOGUE II

JACOB

Two years later...

I never tired of watching Lila play with Rosemary, our little girl. Lila was still a toddler, and a little ungainly – in an adorable sort of way - when she walked.

Rosemary was only a little under a year old, but she loved nothing more than to walk around while holding onto the sides of whatever table or couch was near, laughing wildly as Lila hurried around her.

She wasn't the only baby in the picture. Laura and Archie had one of their own – though their little boy, Jonas, was only a few months old and not nearly big enough to play with the girls.

We were all gathered at the Malibu house, a BBQ going as Delilah, Maryann, Corrine and Laura all talked next to the pool. Archie was there, along with Sam, who had solved his money woes and was preparing to take full custody of Lila once more.

He'd done well since Naomi had been out of the picture.

I sipped my beer, thinking back to that unpleasant time when I'd cornered her at her home with hard evidence that she'd paid someone from Sam's business to pull a hit and run on Delilah and me.

We'd learned the motive, too – she'd assumed that I would be the one driving the car and had instructed her "assistant" to slam head-on into the driver's side.

Turns out she'd wanted to take me out of the picture, or at least scare me enough to back off and leave Delilah alone for her to work her magic on.

Hadn't turned out that way.

We'd given her an ultimatum – leave LA for good, never to come back, and we wouldn't press charges. Lila would be raised by Sam and her sisters, and if she wanted her mother back in her life, she'd make the decision as an adult.

Naomi might've been cruel and blackhearted, but she'd at least seen the wisdom of taking that option rather than facing a trial for attempted murder. Last we heard; she was in New York trying to find the next man to put the screws to.

In LA, life was perfect. Delilah and I were married, and she was expecting baby number two. This one, however, we were going to wait until the day of birth to find out the sex.

Delilah was kicking ass in life, just as I'd expected. She was in the middle of her master's program, and when she completed that, the plan was to take a little time off, focus on motherhood a bit before thinking about her Ph.D.

Her investments were also blossoming, and she was already thinking about new ones to make.

Cherry Lane was still a smash, though I'd stepped back from running things as hands-on as I had before. Instead of opening a second location in Vegas, I'd decided to stick around and try something new in LA.

Archie was the manager of Cherry Lane in all but name, while I was the GM of Lush, a new club in downtown LA that was more traditional – drinking and dancing, but nothing too risqué. Already it was the talk of the town, and rarely a weekend went by without one A-lister or another stopping in for a visit.

Needless to say, it was wildly profitable.

I sipped my beer, my train of thought derailed by Helen's entrance. She'd recently purchased a condo in Santa Monica, which meant she was able to split her time between LA and London.

She was a wonderful grandmother, and I was damn pleased to know that our children would be growing up surrounded by so much love.

I set down my drink and stepped over to Delilah as she stood by the pool, wrapping my arms around her waist from behind and kissing her on the cheek.

"Hey there, handsome," she said, kissing me back.

The evening was perfect, the weather warm and just right for some family fun in the pool. Dinner would be ready in a bit, and I was getting good and hungry.

"Have I ever told you how damn happy I am? How much l love you?"

She smiled warmly at me.

"You might've mentioned it once or twice. Doesn't mean I don't like hearing it again. And I love you, too."

I watched Rosemary as she grabbed Helen's legs and pulled herself up. She had Delilah's blue eyes, and my dark hair.

She also had love from the both of us that would carry her through the rest of her life.

The End

Printed in Great Britain
by Amazon

16421305R00140